THE SLEEPING WITNESS

FIORELLA DE MARIA

The Sleeping Witness

A Father Gabriel Mystery

IGNATIUS PRESS   SAN FRANCISCO

Cover images © iStockphoto

Cover design by John Herreid

© 2017 Ignatius Press, San Francisco
All rights reserved
ISBN 978-1-62164-076-9 (PB)
ISBN 978-1-68149-740-2 (eBook)
Library of Congress Control Number 2016934526
Printed in the United States of America ♾

In loving memory of
Fr Dominic Rolls
(1963–2016)

Acknowledgments

I would like to take this opportunity to thank the Benedictine community of Chilworth Abbey, Surrey, especially Prior Benedict, for patiently answering my many questions about monastic life and the vanished world of postwar England.

I

Father Gabriel never felt the slow encroachment of middle age more painfully than on an evening such as this. It was worse than that dusting of silver over his once-black hair that he could no longer ignore or that mild ache in his joints when he awoke on cold mornings. It was even worse than the need he felt to hold books and papers at arm's length as long-sightedness crept up at him and he continued to tell himself that he could do without reading glasses a little longer yet.

Gabriel was seated at his favourite spot in his favourite room of the abbey—the library—and had virtually claimed this particular desk as his own. Not that Gabriel believed in ownership of any kind, of course, but this gnarled, old oak desk, etched in many places with the graffiti of novices past, had come to feel more like an old friend than an inanimate object during the years of his formation at Saint Mary's Abbey.

His Truth shall compass thee with a shield: thou shalt not be afraid of the terror of the night. Of the arrow that flieth in the day, of the business that walketh about in the dark; of invasion, or of the noonday devil. A thousand shall fall at thy side, and ten thousand at thy right hand.

It was his ability to concentrate that was beginning to let him down; his eyes wandered from the safety of the Holy Scriptures opened up before him and looked out the leaded window. Gabriel could not deny the other reason he loved this place. From where he was sitting, he was completely concealed from view should anyone enter through the library door; if he were alert enough, he could lower his eyes again in a moment should he hear the telltale squeak of the hinges. The words upon which he had been struggling to focus lay forgotten as Gabriel glanced longingly at the gardens below. He would do his penance later. The outside world was so very beautiful at this hour of the day, when the summer sun was only just starting to flicker and fade. From his vantage point, he could admire every detail: the lush herb garden where Brother Gerard knelt, yanking out weeds from among the delicate stems with a combination of precision and mild aggression; the mosaic of vegetable plots that had been impressive lawns before it had become necessary to Dig for Victory—victory had come but they were still digging while food remained scarce. The monks had reclaimed one stretch of ground for grass in the past year, and it sloped in lush green brilliance down to the distant apple orchard, where he would no doubt find employment when the autumn came.

Concentrate! The voice of Gabriel's conscience always managed to sound like the abbot at his most indignant, and he looked down at the page again, to no avail. Through his head ran images of apples, barrels and barrels of the things from the heaving branches. He could almost smell the overpowering boozy scent of the cider press. *A thousand shall fall at thy side . . . a thousand . . . a thousand.*

He shook his head and looked back at the inviting window, down at the rosebushes that marked the end of the lawn in a riot of red and white splendour. Behind the roses, he could just make out a woman walking along the path from the orchard. Her hat obscured much of her face from view, but he recognised her immediately as Marie Paige, the village doctor's wife. She had an unusually slow gait for a young woman and walked as though she really were treading on eggshells, every step deliberate and a little hesitant. Every so often, she would stop altogether to catch her breath.

Thou shalt not be afraid of the terror of the night.

During one of her pauses, Marie glanced up at the window with the finely tuned instinct of a woman who is used to being watched. Much to his embarrassment, Gabriel found himself looking directly into her face, their eyes locking before he could turn away. He raised a hand in greeting and tried to make it look as though he had only just glanced out the window, not that she could possibly have known either way. He waited for her gloved hand to flutter back before returning to his study, guiltily aware of his lapse.

"Gabriel! What are you doing?"

Gabriel jumped. It was not the abbot-like voice of his conscience rebuking him this time; it was Abbot Ambrose in person, as large as life and as irascible as ever. Unusually for Gabriel, he had been so distracted that he had failed to hear the warning squeak of the door and the abbot's cadaverous figure had appeared at his side before he could tear himself away from the window. "Gabriel," he repeated, as though he were addressing a recalcitrant schoolboy—which was exactly how Gabriel was behaving. "What are you doing?"

"Forgive me, Father Abbot," murmured Gabriel, turning to look at him, "I was only resting for a moment. Then I noticed a figure in the grounds."

Abbot Ambrose narrowed his eyes. Even when he was standing at ease (the word "relaxed" scarcely applied), Ambrose's bald head wore the look of a gentleman who could kill a rival at ten paces, and Gabriel felt himself looking hastily away. "That's a lie, you were watching that woman a full five minutes before you waved at her."

"How did you know I was looking at a woman?" *It is written all over my face!* he thought. *I am probably as red as a beetroot.*

"Because I observed her myself from the other window as I entered the room," growled Ambrose. "Mrs Paige really ought to be discouraged from wandering about the grounds like that."

"No one has the heart, she always looks so sad." Gabriel had a nasty feeling that he was digging himself ever further into a hole from which only the abbot would be able to extricate him. He changed tack as skilfully as he could. "There's an ugly rumour—"

"We would not be listening to malicious gossip now, would we?" There was an unmistakeable threat to the abbot's tone that prompted Gabriel to shut his mouth on the subject. "I am fully aware of Mr Merriott's little story, but there have been quite a few of those over the years. I will not have Dr Paige's good name sullied without evidence."

"I'm sorry, Father Abbot."

And Gabriel, who was not afraid of very much these days —night terrors or arrows or even the noonday devil, when it came to it—was very much afraid of making a mess of things and turned to Ambrose to ask for penance. He knew he should not have noticed her in the garden, and he had given away that he had observed her rather too often. Worse, perhaps, as Abbot Ambrose obviously knew, Gabriel *had* been listening to gossip and had half believed Gordon Merriott's claims, not because he thought ill of Dr Paige but because Marie really did look as though she lived in a state of permanent fear. Worst of all, he became aware that Abbot Ambrose had stopped talking and Gabriel had no idea what penance he had been given—if any—because he had been too distracted to hear. At the risk of being ticked off for being overscrupulous, he would now have to ask penance for becoming distracted whilst being given a penance for becoming distracted, and Abbot Ambrose had never been the sort of man who appreciated having to repeat himself.

2

Two weeks later, the abbey grounds were a hive of activity, and for once, nobody minded who wandered about or who noticed. It was the feast of the Assumption, the abbey's patronal feast and a garden party was in full swing. To alleviate the continuing problems caused by rationing, everyone in the village was invited along with the request that they bring some contribution to the feast. Social activities were few and far between in a village like Sutton Westford, and the abbey grounds were exceptionally beautiful in the middle of summer. It was therefore no surprise that virtually anyone who could be there—sceptics, agnostics and atheists included—had appeared by midday, armed with plates and tins and baskets of food.

"This is a waste of a sunny afternoon," commented Gordon Merriott, as he loped to one of the tables with a tray he had been requested to carry. "In my humble opinion."

"Well, since you're so humble, we won't ask your opinion," Brother Gerard retorted, taking the tray from him as though he could not trust the man not to hide it up his sleeve. Gerard threw himself into the task of finding space for the various items on the already laden table. "Don't be such an old bore."

"Bloody Scousers."

"As a matter of fact, I'm from Preston. Don't you southern nancies know the difference?"

An elderly woman appeared between them. "Please, no fighting."

Gerard had a mild allergy to old ladies at the best of times and groaned without meaning to. "We are not fighting, Mrs Webb, only having a friendly disagreement."

Mrs Webb aimed a prim look at him from beneath her battered straw hat. "Brother Gerard, you be more friendly then."

Gerard chuckled as Gordon Merriott shook his head and moved away in search of somebody else to bait. "Tell that to Thomas Becket. Sorry Mrs Webb, but he always eats more than anyone else and moans about being here in the first place."

Gordon Merriott glared over his shoulder. "It's all right, Brother, I'll get the rest of the sandwiches. Don't get up."

Gerard's laughter died in his throat but his smile did not waver. At a mere five foot four and wiry to boot, he was unlikely ever to grow into a towering giant in spite of his youth, but he had trained himself not to be troubled by the handicap a long time ago and took every jibe in the best humour he could muster. "Good things come in small packages, Merriott."

"So does poison," he answered, without missing a beat.

Gerard turned round to see Gabriel moving determinedly in his direction, never a sight that boded well at the best of times. "What have I done? What have I said . . . ?"

"Whoever you're in trouble with, it's not me for once," answered Gabriel jovially, "I'm the one who's been up to my neck in it. I'm astonished I've been allowed out to join the party."

"Dissipation, Dom Gabriel," creaked Gerard, sounding more like Victor Frankenstein's assistant than Abbot Ambrose.

"Could you please start organising some games for the children before Father Abbot bursts a blood vessel? The hot weather's not helping his temper and one of the boys has already been caught trying to drink the cider."

Gerard gave a wry smile. "Do I get to chat with the grown-ups when I'm bigger?"

"Just go away!" Gabriel's attention was drawn to a small gaggle of men and women sipping drinks near the path where guests always entered. A tall, ungainly young man he had never met before stooped a little to talk to the woman next to him. "What an odd face he has," he inadvertently mused out loud. "He looks like a good-looking man who's been hit by a bus."

"Charming observation."

"You know what I mean, his face looks *squashed* somehow. All his features are too close together."

"You'd better be nice to him, he's a war hero," said Gerard in a low voice. "Mrs Webb was telling me the other day. He's come over from Denmark for the summer to paint pictures." Gabriel glanced sidelong at Gerard. "It's true, he's an artist."

"Is he indeed?"

"Yeah, he's rented Hilltop Cottage so as he can get some peace and quiet to paint about his war experiences."

"Wonder what he's doing here then?" But Gerard had walked away, leaving Gabriel talking to himself. He looked around at the people milling about and knew all of them in some way or another. Most attended Mass on Sundays, many of the children came to the abbey for catechism; others he knew from the months he had spent living in the village before he had plucked up the courage to enter the abbey as a postulant. Only the Danish artist was a stranger, and he felt a natural curiosity to speak with him further.

"Look at that!" It was Mrs Webb at his elbow, pointing in the direction of Dr Paige and his wife who had just arrived. Mrs Webb was the sort of old lady whose vocation in life was to affirm the celibacy of every priest and religious in her vicinity. Gabriel felt his impatience rising immediately.

"What am I supposed to be looking at?"

"Look at them!"

Gabriel did just that. "A young couple arrive at a garden party arm in arm, dressed in their best, chatting happily together. Was there something else I should have spotted?"

"Oh Father! He never leaves her alone."

"As a matter of fact, I see Mrs Paige walking alone quite often."

"Yes, when the doctor is busy." Mrs Webb's voice had taken on a conspiratorial whisper that made Gabriel want someone to hurl a firecracker in his direction, just to cause a diversion. "But when they're together, always he is fussing, always *watching*."

"Mrs Webb, she is obviously unwell. He is quite rightly very solicitous after her. I think it's allowed."

Dr Paige had passed Marie a glass of cordial before helping himself to some wine. She hovered in front of the plates of food, apparently unable to decide what to try first or perhaps too dainty to show any enthusiasm. Finally, Dr Paige picked a neat, white triangle of cucumber sandwich and handed it to her, making a half-joking apology for handling it. Even Gabriel had to admit that this last gesture looked a little odd, but he was reassured by Marie's unusually talkative manner. The two of them chatted easily with the guests around them —the sandwich never going near Marie's mouth—unaware that they were a subject of conversation. "You know what people say," volunteered Mrs Webb. "That's why he never lets her talk to anyone unless he's with her. Afraid she'll tell on him."

"They're a perfectly nice couple, madam. Leave them in peace."

Gabriel made for the food table with Mrs Webb still at his elbow, but he thought he might throw her off once they reached the rest of the gathering. He purposefully began a conversation with Dr Paige and was relieved to find that it did the trick. Mrs Webb turned her attention to Marie and appeared to Gabriel to be intent upon rescuing the poor waif from the ministrations of her overbearing husband. As he reached for a glass, Gabriel overheard Mrs Webb employing all her gifts of subtlety: "Come with me, my dear. You need some fresh air . . ."

"I'm glad you could take some time off, Dr Paige," said Gabriel, half glancing at the doctor, half searching for Mrs Webb and Marie. "How is your wife? She looks a little pale."

Dr Paige shrugged. "She's not been well, but she's getting stronger every day. You know how it is."

Gabriel had no idea but smiled anyway. "All credit to you, no doubt."

"Well, I hope I'm doing more good than ill." Dr Paige took a sip of his wine. Like many men whose youth had been brought to an abrupt end by the outbreak of war, his physical appearance did not match his demeanour in the slightest. To look at him, Dr Paige was a dapper young man of modest means, still at a stage in his life where he seemed to be self-consciously trying to look like one of the grown-ups. It jarred somehow with his world-weary manner. He was not depressed, thought Gabriel, he was not the sort of character to go around getting depressed about anything, but like his wife he just seemed, well, *sad*. Perhaps it was as simple as that—sad—or even distracted, as though someone had put his whole life in shadow and he could not remember how it felt to have the sunshine on his face.

Gabriel's musings were brought to an abrupt halt by a sudden commotion behind him. Dr Paige looked over Gabriel's shoulder in alarm before pushing past him; Gabriel turned around and saw a circle of fretting figures with Mrs Webb the most audible of them all, calling: "Please! Give her some air!"

At a closer look, he realised Marie had collapsed, so suddenly that the people around her had only just had time to stop her head hitting the ground. He heard the smash of her glass being trodden underfoot and Dr Paige demanding that he be allowed to get close to her.

"Let him pass!" called Gabriel, but the huddle of men and women were already parting to let Dr Paige through. Gabriel could just make out the reed-like outline of Marie's limp body surrounded by worried, curious, thoroughly useless observers. Dr Paige lifted her in his arms with the assurance of a man who had carried his wife like that many times; he glanced in Gabriel's direction. "It's all right, she's just a little hot. May I take her inside?"

He moved in the direction of the building without awaiting an answer and was soon joined by Fr Dominic, the infirmarian, keen to help—and Mrs Webb, keen not to miss out. "Does the lady need to lie down?" said Fr Dominic, struggling to keep up. He walked with a pronounced limp due to childhood polio and was no match for Dr Paige's easy strides, even though Dr Paige carried a grown woman in his arms.

"No, no, that won't be necessary," said Dr Paige. "She just needs somewhere quiet to sit until her head clears. It's all right, happens all the time."

In the welcome cool of indoors, Dr Paige laid Marie on the floor on a jacket another guest had kindly lent him. She showed no signs of coming round. "Should I ring for an ambulance?" suggested Gabriel. "She's awfully white."

"It looks worse than it is," Dr Paige assured him. "She'll be quite all right in a minute or two. Just a moment—" He was distracted by the sight of Mrs Webb trying to remove Marie's jacket. "What do you think you're doing?"

"She's too hot," said Mrs Webb by way of an explanation. "I wonder if she is expecting.—" Mrs Webb fell silent—a most unusual occurrence—her gaze fixed on Marie's now bare arm. "She's hurt," she gasped, but from where Gabriel stood he could not see what she was looking at.

Dr Paige covered his wife's arm again with a sudden rush of anger. "I don't recall asking for your assistance, Mrs Webb," he snapped, but his attention was taken by the sight of Marie starting to tremble. A moment later, she began to move her head and open her eyes. "It's all right, my love," he said quietly, "you've just taken a bit of a turn. It's all right."

Gabriel heard a familiar, uneven tread and looked round to see Dominic shuffling in their direction, carrying a glass tumbler of something medicinal. "Sorry it has taken me a while," said Dominic, giving Dr Paige the awkward smile of a man who is destined to be late for every crisis. "I thought you might need some brandy for the lady."

"Much obliged, Father, thank you."

Gabriel and Dominic watched as Dr Paige cradled his wife's head in the crook of his arm and pressed the glass to her lips. "It's all right, it's only a drop of brandy," he told her, "something to revive you. That's it."

Marie sipped the brandy resignedly then looked up at the two black figures at her side. She suppressed the instinct well, but Gabriel could not help noticing her shrinking away before she recalled who they were. "I'm awfully sorry," she said haltingly, "I've ruined the party, haven't I?"

"Of course you haven't," promised Dominic, shaking his silver-grey head, "it's a frightfully hot day. I dare say you were a little thirsty. Why don't you rest indoors for a little while?"

"Will you look after her while I walk home and fetch the car?" Dr Paige asked Gabriel. "I'd better take her home."

"There's no need," said Marie, taking her husband's hand with the intention of getting up. He did not seem to realise what she wanted and made no effort to help her stand. "I'm quite all right now, don't let's——"

But Dr Paige was on his feet, leaving Gabriel to help Marie up. "Darling, I insist. You're not well, you need rest." He made for the door without further word, stopping only to say to Gabriel, "I shan't be long. She's in no state to walk home."

Marie, now standing unsteadily, looked visibly embarrassed. "I'm sorry, he worries far too much. I'll take a little walk around the garden if you don't mind."

"Are you sure you wouldn't rather rest inside a little longer?" suggested Dominic. "Your hands are trembling."

Marie clenched her fists as though commanding her body to pull itself together. "A little fresh air is all I need. Thank you, you have been most kind."

Dominic and Gabriel watched anxiously as Marie walked outside, her stick-like silhouette hovering a moment in the doorway before she disappeared into the garden. "Why was she shaking like that?" asked Gabriel. "She looked as though she'd seen a ghost."

"Her blood pressure's still a little low after fainting," said Dominic absently, looking in the direction Marie had walked. "And she's very fair to be out in the sun on a hot day."

"Mrs Webb thinks she's expecting."

"I very much doubt it. Can't really imagine a creature as frail as that carrying a baby somehow."

"Ought I to go after her?" Neither man said it, but both knew that if anyone needed to walk anywhere quickly and discreetly, it was not going to be Dominic.

"Leave her," said Dominic, "Mrs Webb is wrong about virtually everything, but she is right about Dr Paige; he is too possessive. There was no need for him to walk all the way home, drive back here and whisk his wife home to her sickbed because she became a little overheated."

"He said to look after her."

"I hardly think Mrs Paige requires a chaperone—or even desires one by the way she made herself scarce just then." Dominic threw Gabriel a warning look. "Brace yourself," he murmured under his breath.

A second later, Mrs Webb was at Gabriel's side, red-eyed and crestfallen. "There was no reason for the doctor to be so sharp with me," she whined, "I was only trying to help! When a woman faints she needs to cool down—"

"No need to worry, Mrs Webb," said Dominic, coming to Gabriel's rescue. "You did the right thing. Dr Paige was a little anxious about his wife's health, that's why he snapped. No need to take it personally."

"He doesn't care about her at all!" she burst out. "She has big bruises on her arm! He was angry because I saw them!"

"Mrs Webb, please! I didn't see anything!" protested Gabriel. "You can't make an accusation like that—"

"You didn't see anything, but I did! As big as a man's fist, they were."

Gabriel turned to Dominic for support but was disconcerted by his friend's silence. Instead of backing him up, Dominic stood listening anxiously to the woman as though he were actually taking her seriously. "Dominic?"

"No one ever listens to me!" continued Mrs Webb relentlessly. "You men are all the same, always you defend each other! Listen then to Gordon Merriott."

Gabriel closed his eyes, longing for once for the sound of a bell to ring to bring this ordeal by social nicety to an end.

As Gordon Merriott's latest round of rumourmongering was being discussed, the man himself had partaken of as much refreshment as even he could manage and gone off on his own to have a quiet cigarette. He stood under a tree at the nearest edge of the apple orchard, positioning himself so as to make the most of the shade it offered. All in all, it was pleasantly cool, and he could hear the lazy murmur of bees humming around the nearby rosebushes; that, and the blissfully distant sounds of human conversation.

He heard the crack of twigs breaking underfoot and started slightly. No reason why there should not be others walking around the orchard if he had thought to come this way; but only the monks were supposed to walk there, and he could sense by the urgency of the footsteps that whatever man was walking past him on the other side of the tree, he was trespassing and knew it. Gordon stubbed out his cigarette so that the curl of smoke would not give him away and listened intently.

There were two people talking, a man and a woman. For a moment he could not make out what they were saying; then his brain registered that they were speaking German and began to decipher the words. Having been taken prisoner during the Great War, Merriott's understanding of German was virtually fluent; but the long years had taken their toll, and he struggled with the laborious process of translating the conversation in his head.

"Why have you come here?" It was the woman, distressed, almost pleading. "For pity's sake leave me alone!"

"I had to find you, Marie, I had to know if you were alive."

"Please go away! I can't bear to look at you!"

"Come to me! Don't make me search for you among the crowds, my love. Don't make me come for you—"

"Stop it!"

"I haven't had you for such a long time, Marie——"

"Don't touch me! My husband will be here any minute, he's gone to fetch the car . . ."

"I cannot believe you married him."

"Well I did marry him, Johannes, I have a life of my own now. You will not take it from me, you've taken everything else!"

Gordon held his breath, not daring to blink as Marie Paige rushed past, shaking with emotion. He had never thought her capable of moving that quickly. In the distance, he could see Dr Paige parking his motorcar and knew she must be trying to return to the party before he arrived and found her missing. "Well, well, well, Mrs Paige," chuckled Gordon, reaching into his pocket for another cigarette. "But who could blame you, eh?"

Gordon was so preoccupied with the tasks of striking a match and congratulating himself on his own cleverness that he forgot completely that the other half of the couple had not yet left.

3

The next morning dawned cool and clear, but with blue skies promising another balmy day. Dr Paige's army background had left him with a lifelong dependence upon routine, and he left his home every morning at exactly the moment the grandfather clock in the hall chimed the half hour. He had calculated, when he and his wife had first purchased the cottage, that it was a twelve-minute brisk walk from the front gate to the surgery. If he left the house half an hour before he was due to start work, it allowed him six minutes to pop into the village shop and buy a newspaper (making allowances for the inevitable small talk he would be expected to make as he paid). He could, of course, have arranged to have the morning paper delivered, but he preferred the absolute control of going to the shop himself and purchasing it at the most convenient possible time to going through the irritation of awaiting the arrival of the paper boy. The extra five minutes in the morning routine were a contingency for any conversation into which me might be dragged as he walked through the sleepy streets, but which could also be used to catch a quick glimpse at the day's headlines if he were lucky enough to get from front door to surgery without anyone stopping to talk to him.

On good mornings, Dr Paige would be woken by the sound of Marie downstairs preparing breakfast. He would hear the fairy-soft sound of her slippered feet on the creaking wooden floorboards, the whistle of the kettle, the clank of plates and cups being laid out on the pine table. On not such good mornings, Dr Paige would slide noiselessly out of bed to avoid waking his exhausted wife, pussyfoot about the room getting dressed, then make his own breakfast, leaving a portion for Marie in a covered dish as a hint that she should remember to eat.

That morning had not been a good one for Marie, but Dr Paige had known things would be difficult after her latest episode and was determined not to let it trouble him unduly. She was exhausted and needed rest. That extra hour in the morning would see her through until after lunch, when the bulk of the household chores were done and she could lie down again for an hour if necessary before embarking upon the task of cooking the evening's meal.

He pushed open the glass-fronted door of the village shop and listened for the tinny clang of the bell overhead, which warned Reggie McClusker to come out of the back room to the counter. Not that he needed warning at that time of the morning, when a steady stream of customers came in and out on their way to work or school to buy sweets, cigarettes or journals and Reggie was on permanent sentry duty dispensing change and goodies. Within the hour, the housewives would start queuing and bartering for food. "Morning, Doctor! How's your missus this morning?"

"Much better, thank you," answered Dr Paige, handing him the paper he had picked up. "Another day's rest and she'll be as right as rain."

"Good to hear. Nothing serious I hope. Out of the way, sonny!"

The boy Reggie had roared at, face partially covered by his school cap, hurried in the direction of the door. "Don't be too hard on him, Reg," said Dr Paige, placing a coin on the counter. "He can't help being a bit clumsy."

"He can in my shop. Have a good day."

~

Two hours later, after he had said his Mass and changed into clericals, Gabriel left the monastery armed with a large basket and began his walk to the village shop. As chores went, Gabriel felt it was the most pleasant he could have been given, allowing him a precious hour of relative liberty whilst giving anyone who might need his assistance the chance to approach him. Like Dr Paige (who might not have felt altogether uncomfortable in a monastery), Gabriel had a routine that was unwavering, and the rest of the village knew that they could walk that particular route at that time of day and pretend accidentally to have bumped into him. That way anyone who needed to do so could talk to him or ask his advice without going through the awkward formality of making an appointment, as long as they did not mind walking alongside him and occasionally taking turns to carry the basket.

On this unremarkable morning, it was Alastair Brennan he met, almost as soon as he had turned in the direction of the village, but on this occasion he suspected the meeting was a genuine accident. Alastair Brennan was one of those effortlessly handsome men whose looks had the nerve to-get better not worse with age. As such, it was difficult to place him, though Gabriel deduced from the fact that he had served during the War that he could not be much older than forty. He was one of the War's many invalids, but he was known to joke that a paralysed left arm was a good enough exchange for the modest pension that kept him solvent between royalties cheques.

"Good morning, Father!" he called, giving Gabriel a cheery wave. "Out nice and early I see."

"Good morning, Mr Brennan. I've been up for hours."

Alastair caught up with Gabriel and got into stride next to him. "Sorry, I forgot it's the middle of the afternoon for you chaps. Love the early morning myself, but I don't know how you get up at the crack of dawn every single day."

"At least at this time of year it *is* the crack of dawn," mused Gabriel. "It's never quite so easy to get up in the dark. How's the book coming along?"

"Not at all well, Father," Alastair confessed. "They say that there's no such thing as writer's block, but I beg to differ. Sorry I was not at your bash the other day, by the way. I had to go up to town."

"I see. Still there, is it?" Gabriel had grown up in London and still had wistful feelings for leafy Finchley during idle moments, but he doubted that the house in which he had grown up was still there after the Luftwaffe's many visits to the region.

"I gather there was a bit of a drama. Marie all right, is she?"

"Ladies faint on occasion. It was hardly the first time— for Marie or the Assumption Day garden party, I suspect."

They had reached the row of cottages at the edge of the village. Some way in front of them, a woman walked very slowly across the road, pausing only to catch her breath. She was too far away to notice them, but Gabriel placed a hand on Alastair's arm to indicate that he should stand still. "Why not go to her?" he whispered to Gabriel.

"Because Mrs Paige evidently does not wish to be seen."

"How can you tell that from so far away?"

"From the way her head keeps turning to look around her, as though she is ensuring she is not being followed."

Alastair shook his head. "She always does that. Nervous habit, poor little thing." The moment had passed. Gabriel and Alastair hesitated a little longer to make absolutely sure they would not intercept her, then continued on their way past the houses, past the school and finally to the desultory little huddle of shops that made up the high street.

Inside Reggie's shop, Alastair waited by the counter whilst Gabriel requested matches and sugar. "Surprised you haven't worked out how to produce your own yet, Father," remarked Reggie, taking the stack of ration books Gabriel handed him. "I'm a bit low on sugar—half the village has taken their ration this morning. You need to come earlier."

"Well, I shall have to ask Father Abbot to excuse me Prime so that I can cadge the monastic share of sugar," Gabriel remarked, then regretted his tone. "Just give me what you can spare, Reggie."

The bell clanked and Gordon Merriott burst in with a triumphant look on his face. "I just seen Mrs Paige creeping along the road."

Gabriel swallowed an irritable retort but Alastair spared him the trouble. "You can't have just seen anything, Merriott," snapped Alastair, "we both saw her at least fifteen minutes ago."

"Aw, don't split hairs. Fifteen minutes is just seen." Gordon Merriott leant towards Reggie, sensing that his old friend would offer more encouragement than the others. "You'll never guess what I overheard at that posh party?"

"I'm sure we do not need to know," Gabriel began, but he could sense Reggie's eagerness. "Tittle tattle lost the battle."

"War's over, mate," answered Gordon, as though that solved a problem. "A little quarrel between love birds, hiding away in the orchard no less."

"That's enough!" demanded Gabriel. "Whatever you heard was none of your business and certainly not meant for our ears."

"Oh don't you fret, Father," Reggie put in. "I hear more filth in this place than you do in the confessional. Only most times no one ain't sorry."

"Nevertheless—"

"I understand the lingo, you see." Gordon put on the dreamy voice of a lovestruck youth. " 'Don't make me search for you among the crowds, my love. Don't make me come for you' and all that rubbish. Then she's begging him to leave her alone. 'I'm married . . . !' "

"Merriott!"

"Foreign artist bloke and you'll never guess who?"

"Stop it!"

"Mrs Butter-wouldn't-melt-in-her-mouth, the village waif herself. *Oi!*"

Gordon would not have been able to duck out of the way of Alastair's right fist in time, had Gabriel not attempted to hold the man off. "Out of my way, Father, I'll beat his head in!"

Alastair was a well-built man and still in possession of considerable strength in spite of his disability, but Gabriel was similarly proportioned and gave Alastair a shove in the direction of the door. He told himself afterwards that he was only slightly taking advantage of the man's infirmity and his unwillingness to risk striking a man of the cloth, but somehow or other he managed to hustle Alastair out into the street before he could do Gordon any harm. "Have you taken leave of your senses?" hissed Gabriel, marching him around a corner so that they were out of the sight of yet more nosy parkers. "Don't give him the pleasure of provoking you."

"The pleasure would have been entirely mine, Father!" roared Alastair, scarlet with rage. "Dickie and Marie Paige are very dear friends of mine. I will not have their names sullied by scum like Merriott!"

"Sssh! Keep your voice down or you'll do his job for him!" pleaded Gabriel, glancing around. There was no one obviously within earshot, but that evidently counted for very little if Gordon Merriott was anything to go by. "No one listens to Merriott. There's not a character in the village he hasn't tried to drag through the mud, it's the sort of poisonous man he is."

"I don't care who else he's hurt," hissed Alastair, "if he does anything to harm Marie, I'll tear his miserable little carcass into pieces. I am not making an idle threat."

"I sincerely hope you are, this is uncalled for!" Gabriel knew it was nothing in the least. The harm Gordon Merriott did was intolerable, and he knew from bitter experience that mud had a tendency to stick. He tried a lighter tack. "Don't you remember the time he had some poor chap arrested for burglary? Turned out it was the man's elderly mother's house and he was breaking in through a window because she'd lost her keys and couldn't get in!"

Alastair was not to be placated. "That was an unfortunate mistake, this is sheer malice. Marie has enough problems without that swine stirring up the village against her. I won't stand by and see it done."

Gabriel watched passively as Alastair Brennan stalked off down the road. He knew he should do something: warn Marie Paige if nothing else or try to talk to Gordon, though he did not imagine that would help. Rumours were so difficult to fight. He thought of the old story of Philip Neri, who was supposed to have told a gossiping woman to pluck a chicken and scatter the feathers through the town, only to instruct her afterwards to pick up every single feather she had scattered. Gabriel knew he would never be able to pick up the feathers Gordon Merriott had scattered about over the years. He walked back in the direction of Reggie's shop to collect his basket, the ration books and whatever Reggie was able to sell him, calculating how long he had before he had to be back at the abbey and how quickly he could perform his errands. In the end, Gabriel decided to risk being late in the interests of helping a woman in distress and went in search of Marie.

He had guessed correctly that Marie had been on her way back from an errand when she had crossed his path earlier, which partly explained how out of breath she had been. Whatever she had been doing, she had been on her feet longer than was altogether wise and by the time he had caught sight of her, she had already started suffering for the overexertion. When Gabriel knocked on the door of her cottage, he saw Marie's anxious face peer through the front window before the sound of faltering steps heralded the opening of the door.

"Good morning, Father," she greeted him with forced brightness. She looked more than usually wan, he thought, her already sunken face sharper than ever with grey smudges under her eyes from lack of sleep. Nevertheless, she had made some effort that morning; her short hair was carefully combed, and though she wore no make-up, her dress was neat and presentable.

"Good morning, Mrs Paige, I was just passing. I thought I'd see how you were."

"I'm quite well, thank you."

"Good." He sensed her reluctance to let him in, but stood his ground. "Your husband is also well?"

"Yes thank you, he is well."

"Good."

Marie stepped back as though admitting defeat. "Do come in, Father, you must be tired."

Gabriel stepped past her into the hall before she could find an excuse to close the door in his face. "Well, I wouldn't say no to sitting down for a moment."

"Come in then. I'll put the kettle on."

Marie showed Gabriel into the sitting room and gestured for him to take a seat. It was a small but pleasant room with a large, south-facing sash window and several mahogany bookcases crammed with books. He sat in an armchair near the fireplace and cast his eye over the Bechstein piano sitting open in the far corner. "You play?"

"Yes, my husband encourages it. I sometimes accompany him when he sings."

Gabriel felt the atmosphere relaxing somewhat. "I didn't know he sang. He's a man of many talents."

"He has a fine bass voice," Marie volunteered, giving a rare smile. "He was a choral scholar at Cambridge before his conversion. Let me make that tea."

"No," replied Gabriel, seizing the moment. He had noted the time on the clock as they walked through the hall and knew he was doomed to the wrath of the abbot, but there was no call for being so late that they sent out search parties for him. "I—I can't stay long. Why don't you sit down?"

Marie perched gingerly on a chair; Gabriel could almost see the shutters coming down as she did so and suspected he had already missed his opportunity. "I didn't realise your husband was a convert. That must have been Gilbey's work."

Marie rolled her eyes. Gabriel did not find her an easy character to make out, but she did not suffer fools gladly and did not appear to care if he noticed. "I don't think you came here to discuss my husband's conversion to Catholicism, now did you, Father? Would something be the matter?"

"Actually," he said, clearing his throat, "I rather wondered if something were the matter with you? You see, when you fainted—"

"Father, I am perfectly well," she retorted, with the irritation of a woman whose health is a constant cause of enquiry. "I feel very foolish for making such a spectacle of myself. If I had had a moment's warning, I should have sat down or taken a sip of my drink, but I'm afraid it came on very quickly. I felt better almost immediately."

"I see. Forgive me, it was not my intention to interfere."
It was absolutely my intention to interfere, thought Gabriel, but
her guarded tone unnerved him. It was no good, he was going to have to say it. "I'm sorry to say this, Mrs Paige, but
there are rumours swirling about the village. Gossip spreads
very quickly in small communities such as this and—"

"I do not listen to rumours," answered Marie curtly, rising abruptly to her feet, "and I give very short shrift to those
who spread them, men of the cloth included."

"I assure you, I was only trying to—" To his guilty relief, Gabriel saw Marie place a hand to her forehead and
realised that the effect of standing up so suddenly had made
her dizzy. It provided a suitable diversion, and he got up to
help her into the chair he had recently occupied so that she
could sit more comfortably. "I'm so sorry, I didn't mean
to trouble you, but villages can be nasty places at times."
Marie gave a bitter laugh, refusing to meet his eye. "If there
is anything that troubles you, you know you can talk to me,
don't you?"

"I am very much obliged, Father."

As solitary as an oyster, thought Gabriel grimly, getting up
to leave. She was a woman carrying a burden so terrible she
could barely stand it any longer, but she was never going to
share it with him. "I should be going, I have some more
errands to run before I return to the abbey and I am already
very late."

Marie rose to her feet, slowly this time, and escorted him
to the door. "I'm awfully sorry if I sound rude," she said
awkwardly as she opened the door. "I'm afraid I'm not very
good at talking to people. I am not very used to it. No offence, I hope?"

Gabriel smiled warmly. "None at all, I assure you." He hesitated to go, looking fixedly down at the worn stone doorstep. "I meant what I said. Some crosses are impossible to carry alone. If you need to talk to anyone—"

"Thank you, Father," she whispered, causing him to look up at her in surprise. Her face had clouded with emotion, and if it had not been for her change of tone, he would have thought her angry. "If only it were so easy. Who on earth told you that all crosses can be carried by others?"

With that, she closed the door, leaving Gabriel to reproach himself for failing and for deserving Father Abbot's reproach for arriving back for Sext five minutes late.

4

Dr Paige knew something was wrong the second he jolted awake. He lay where he was to be sure he was not dreaming, but he had known before he had opened his eyes that Marie was gone. He could hear neither her shallow, irregular breathing nor the reassuring clatter of breakfast being prepared downstairs. Without sitting up, he reached across to Marie's side of the bed, fingers splayed out, palm facing downwards, and ran his hand along the bedsheet. It was cold. She had left their bed hours ago.

He got up and glanced around the room, noting the untouched sedative on Marie's bedside table. He had prepared it for her as usual the night before, but he remembered now that she had drifted off to sleep before taking it. He had been pleased by the thought that she might not need it any more to get through the night.

It was that detail that sent a usually unflappable man into a panic. He began dressing frantically, not bothering to wash or shave. Never could he remember a moment in their marriage when Marie had deliberately deceived him, but he doubted she had slept at all during the night. For whatever nefarious reason, she had ensured she would be able to get up long before him—possibly to arrive home before he had even noticed—and the sedative would have rendered that impossible.

Minutes later, he staggered down the narrow wooden staircase, a knot of anxiety tightening in his stomach. When he reached the hall, he found a piece of paper crumpled on the floor near the door where it had apparently fallen out of a pocket. A scribbled note, written in a florid, ungainly hand. Dr Paige fell to his knees, ramming it into his trouser pocket before hurtling up the stairs again; he could feel a pulse hammering in his neck.

Shortly afterwards, he was seen leaving his house, pulling the door shut with a slam and marching down the road as though he had the devil at his heels.

The monks were filing out of breakfast—all of them except Gabriel, who had been serving at table and was to have his own breakfast once the refectory was empty. That morning, however, he was destined to go hungry, for as the last of the monks were leaving, the silence was broken by the sound of piercing screams and incoherent shouting. Almost immediately, a small boy in the uniform of the village school came hurtling down the echoing corridor, sobbing hysterically, closely followed by Brother Gerard.

"I'm sorry!" Brother Gerard almost shouted. "He was hammering at the door, screaming hell for leather! I couldn't leave him outside."

"Well, take him somewhere quiet to calm down!" ordered Abbot Ambrose, signalling for Dominic to take charge of the situation. "Fr Gabriel, make yourself useful."

The two men shepherded the child into a quiet room. He was too out of breath to scream any more, but he continued gibbering and crying, too beside himself to speak.

"It's Jimmy, isn't it?" asked Gabriel, crouching down so that he was at eye level with the boy. "You're Mr Mc-Clusker's paper boy, aren't you? I've seen you in the shop."

Jimmy nodded, opened his mouth to speak but only succeeded in bursting into fresh tears.

"It's all right, Jimmy, just tell me what's happened. No one's hurting you."

Jimmy took hold of Gabriel's sleeve, his knuckles white with the effort of calming himself down. "I'm sorry, this was the first place I come to."

"No need to be sorry. What's happened?"

"Murder! There's been a murder."

Gabriel leapt to his feet, yanking his sleeve out of the boy's hand. He had never heard the word spoken directly before and felt a jolt through his body similar to an electric shock. "Where? *Where?*"

"At that foreign bloke's cottage. I heard a gun go off and there they were."

Gabriel did not stop to ask whom he meant, he had a shrewd enough idea. "Look after him!" he called over his shoulder to Dominic, almost colliding with the abbot as he left the room. "Boy says there's been a murder. Let me go and check."

Abbot Ambrose was always on best form during a crisis and simply nodded. "Go, and take Brother Gerard with you. I shall summon help."

Gabriel was a fit man, but Gerard had the advantage of youth and ran ahead, as fast as his short legs and cumbersome habit would allow him. Johannes Pederson's lodge belonged to the abbey and was separated from it by an uneven plot of grassland no more than the size of a playing field, but the men were running uphill on grass still soaked in morning dew. Gabriel could see, as soon as the tumble-down cottage came into view, that the front door was wide open, presumably as Jimmy had left it when he had made the grim discovery and had run screaming to the sanctuary of the abbey.

Gerard disappeared inside, only to come staggering out, seconds later, clutching his head. He leant forwards, retching noisily. The wave of nausea passed as quickly as it had come and he stood up, white and shaking. "There are two of them, Gabriel. Pederson and—Mrs Paige."

Gabriel made a dash for the door, Gerard hovering some way behind him. "Don't touch anything," warned Gabriel, stepping inside. "Be careful."

The smell of blood stuck in his throat, forcing him to stop in his tracks. The next thing he noticed was the state of chaos he had entered. Pederson's cottage consisted of just one large room, with a ladder in the corner leading to a half loft that served as a small bedroom. The ladder, he noticed, had been knocked or kicked and no longer stood straight. The room would once have felt like nothing other than the cosy, bohemian abode of an aspiring artist—paintings un-framed and unmounted leant against the walls, a colourful rug that would recently have covered the bare floorboards lay crumpled and bunched up at one side. What little furni-ture there had been to begin with had been knocked over or pushed out of place during what had clearly been a violent struggle for survival. And in a corner, hunched together in a pool of blood as though they had died in one another's arms, were Marie Paige and Johannes Pederson.

"Sweet Jesus, let this be a dream," murmured Gabriel.

He ran his hand over his eyes before looking again. "Whose blood is that?"

"His," answered Gerard, putting a hand on Gabriel's shoulder. "The boy said he heard a shot; the gun's over there." He indicated a dull metal object partially concealed by shadow behind Johannes' back.

Gabriel knelt at Marie's head. She had been badly battered and he noticed a trickle of blood coming out of her ear where the ear drum must have ruptured with the force of a blow to the side of her head. Her face was so bloodied that if he had not known her, Gabriel was not sure he would have recognised her lying there. "Who would do such a thing?"

In a moment of desperate hope, Gabriel slipped his fingers against the curve of Marie's neck in search of a pulse and, to his immense surprise and relief, he felt the faintest, slowest of rhythms. "Gerard—"

Gerard was standing in the doorway. "Oh, this is bad! Dr Paige is coming."

"Gerard, she's alive."

Gerard spun round. "Are you sure?"

"Only just, but she's definitely alive. Whoever left her for dead didn't stop to check."

Dr Paige appeared in the room, dishevelled and out of breath from running. "Oh my God, someone tell me what's going on!"

Gabriel stepped aside so that Dr Paige could see where Marie was lying, but the doctor froze as soon as he saw the bodies, too paralysed with shock to move. Gabriel waited for him to come to his senses, but he stood rooted to the spot. "Do something!" shouted Gabriel finally, giving the

43

man a shove that nearly knocked him over. "Do something, she's still alive!"

Dr Paige appeared to jolt awake and threw himself down at Marie's side. "Has anyone called an ambulance?" he asked, over his shoulder.

"No, just the police I think," Gerard replied, "the paper boy thought they were both dead."

Dr Paige turned around and glared at them both. "Move! There's very little time!"

Gerard bolted out of the room. Gabriel turned to the doctor, who was removing his jacket to cover Marie. "Dr Paige, I'm so sorry—"

"Not now. You'll need to go down to the road. The ambulance may have trouble finding us."

"Of course."

Gabriel turned to leave. Much later, when discussing the sorry event with the police, he was grateful that middle age was beginning to muddle his memory a little. He forgot all about his reservations about leaving Dr Paige alone at the scene of the crime and clean forgot to tell Inspector Applegate that he had heard the good doctor murmur the words, "Oh God, this is all my fault."

Detective Inspector Applegate stood impassively with his hands firmly planted into his coat pockets as Marie was lifted carefully onto a stretcher and carried outside to the waiting ambulance. He only moved when Dr Paige attempted to follow, raising one hand in his direction as though stopping the traffic. "And where do you think you're going, sir?" he enquired, as though he were talking to Jimmy the paper boy.

"Where does it look as though I'm going?" snapped Dr

Paige, attempting to push past. "Please! I need to be with my wife—surely you can see that?"

Gabriel stepped forwards. "It can't hurt to let him go with her, Inspector, you can find him at the hospital if you need to question him."

"If it's all the same to you, Father," Applegate began and Gabriel wished that for once the words had not come out quite so wrong. He suspected he had just done the doctor the worst possible disservice. "If it's all the same to you, I generally expect murder suspects to come to the station with me, not to meet them at the location of their greatest convenience."

"Murder suspect?" Dr Paige looked frantically in the direction of the two men carrying Marie ever further into the distance. "This is obscene! I arrived here after the monks did, they can tell you that. For pity's sake let me go with my wife, she may be dying!"

"I assure you that there are plenty of doctors and nurses at the hospital to look after your wife, Dr Paige," answered Applegate, tersely. "I'm afraid I need to ask you a few questions about your whereabouts this morning."

Dr Paige looked at Gabriel for support, but Gabriel opened his hands in a gesture of confusion that appeared to rile him more than the inspector's caustic tone. "I'm afraid I have more pressing concerns this morning, Inspector, if you'll excuse me."

Applegate planted himself firmly in the doorway. Somehow, Gabriel was reminded of two boxers squaring up to one another before a match. They were more or less the same height and build though Applegate was of an older generation. Both of them were used to carrying considerable authority, but in this case Dr Paige was in the weaker position and did not seem to know it. "Dr Paige, you can come with me now of your own accord or I can arrest you on suspicion of the attempted murder of Marie Paige and the murder of Johannes Pederson. It's entirely up to you."

Gabriel thought that Applegate would have looked quite impressive at that moment, had he not managed to mispronounce both victims' names, particularly Pederson's, whose name had come out of Applegate's mouth sounding more like Gohan Pedestal. Dr Paige, on the other hand, was comfortably defeated. He turned to Gabriel again. "Please stay with my wife," he pleaded. "I know you have to go back to the abbey, but—"

"I will seek the abbot's permission to go to the hospital," said Gabriel. "Put your mind at rest."

Another well-intentioned comment gone horribly awry between his brain and his mouth, thought Gabriel miserably as he began the walk across the field to the abbey. Dr Paige would never be able to explain how he had come to be in the vicinity of the murder scene when his routine did not normally take him in this direction, and whether or not he had had anything to do with it, Marie would not be woken easily from such a deep sleep. Dr Paige would never have his mind at rest again.

Gabriel's keen sight glimpsed a figure in the distance, walking hurriedly back in the direction of the village. Walking hurriedly was to put it mildly, the man—it could only have been a man—was practically running, taking such vast strides across the grass that Gabriel struggled to focus on his face as his head dipped and rose with the momentum. He was moving with the controlled haste of a person who is badly frightened but whose military training has taught him to remain calm under fire. Gabriel continued to watch the striding figure for any sign that he was about to look up, but Alastair Brennan kept his head down and continued on his way without ever noticing Gabriel's presence.

5

The distressing events of the morning had sent the abbey into such uproar that Gabriel found it refreshingly easy to persuade the abbot to send him on an errand of mercy. Jimmy the paper boy was still being questioned by a constable about what he had seen, though the interview was becoming complicated due to a disagreement over when exactly he had heard the shot fired. As any policeman knew, the passage of time was notoriously difficult for witnesses to calculate, all the more so at moments of extreme panic. There was an unwritten rule that witnesses who knew the exact timings of their every movement and the precise number of minutes that had passed between one horrific event and the next were either liars, fantasists or characters from Agatha Christie stories. The constable half suspected the child had not heard a shot at all and was just adding the detail because he had realised the murder victim had been shot and felt as though he should have heard it.

On his way out of the abbey, Gabriel made a dash for the infirmary to find Dominic. The infirmary sounded grander than it actually was and consisted of a narrow room containing a row of metal-framed beds, one of which had been inhabited for months by Fr Cuthbert, a ninety-eight-year-old man whose memory stretched back as far as the ending of the Crimean War. A stroke had left him too weak to leave his bed or eat without help, but his mind was as clear as ever and he had kept his powers of speech.

"Would you be looking for Fr Dominic?" asked Cuthbert in a muffled tone that reminded Gabriel of a muted violin. "He's gone to fetch something. He'll not be long."

Gabriel chuckled. "Poor Dominic is always long. I'll leave him a message."

"That's right, old chap. I shall look after it if you want."

"Do you have any paper?"

Cuthbert looked askance at him. "Bless me, of course not. Why would I have paper about my person?" His skeletal face split into a mischievous smile that reminded Gabriel unhelpfully of a cheeky medieval *memento mori*, such as he had occasionally come across in old churchyards. "Come now, my son, you would not want this message written down, would you now? You have guilt written all over your face."

That's a bit rich coming from a grinning skull, thought Gabriel. He sighed. "I'm afraid I seem to have a talent for putting my foot in it. I did not do well this morning at all."

"I shouldn't let it trouble you. I landed myself in far more hot water than you ever have when I was still a postulant. But then I was sixteen at the time. One has to make allowances for youth."

Gabriel stepped a little closer to Cuthbert's bedside. "If I tell you the message, will you repeat it to Dominic and no one else? It's important."

Cuthbert's smile faded and was taken over by a look of mild concern. "You're not really in trouble, are you, old chap?"

"Not serious trouble, no. I need you to tell Dominic to meet me at the mortuary as soon as he can. He must come directly."

"The mortuary?"

"Yes. You heard correctly. There's been a murder and I need to ask his advice. You won't forget to tell him, will you?"

Cuthbert closed his eyes thoughtfully. "Well, well, well. Of all the words I expected to hear, murder was not one of them. I'm afraid poor Dominic will not be of much use. He is more used to ministering to the living."

"I need his expert eyes," said Gabriel. "I promise I'm not dragging him into the cauldron with me."

He turned to leave and just had time to hear Cuthbert's parting words: "I hope you will not be jumping into any cauldrons yourself, my son."

Gabriel was not sure whether it was his body or his soul Cuthbert was concerned about, but he told himself all the way down to the village that he was not being wholly disobedient in heading directly to Alastair Brennan's house. He had every intention of going on to the hospital; the mortuary was attached to the hospital after all, and he had instructed Dominic to meet him there as soon as possible. It was just that he knew Dominic would not reach the mortuary for over an hour by the time he had disentangled himself from whatever job he was engaged in and made the cumbersome journey on foot to the hospital. And it was as much an act of mercy to visit Alastair Brennan as Marie Paige, who might well be in less danger—carefully looked after and under constant observation in a hospital—than her unfortunate friend.

Gabriel was taking a short detour to the hospital, nothing more; he was paying a courtesy call to a man who obviously needed assistance in salving his troubled conscience. Gabriel stopped dead outside Brennan's house. He could hear the melodic thunder of a Wagnerian opera crashing through the open window, which he imagined must be driving the neighbours near the point of madness. They would probably have accused him of treason if they had had the faintest clue what it was other than an unbearable racket ruining a summer's morning. He hammered on the door before he could lose his nerve, half expecting Alastair to burst through the front door brandishing a six-foot spear, his head encased in one of those ludicrous horned helmets the Vikings had never worn.

Instead, when the gramophone had been turned off and the door flew open, Gabriel found himself faced with the tall, lanky, faintly unkempt figure he had most definitely seen striding across the fields earlier that day. His face was still ruddy from the exertion, and Gabriel suspected, as the man froze in the doorway, that he had not known whether to open the door or hope that the passerby might do him a favour and go away. "Ah, Fr Gabriel, I wasn't expecting you," he said, with a look of strained surprise. "Do they allow you chaps out in daylight?"

"Only those of us who have reflections in mirrors," Gabriel answered cheerfully. "Might I come in for a moment? I'm on my way to the hospital."

Alastair hesitated in the doorway. "Oughtn't you to go straight to the hospital, Father?" he asked. "There's no knowing how bad things may be for Marie—Mrs Paige. I heard all about it of course. News travels fast."

"It certainly does." Gabriel raised an eyebrow. "I hope for your sake no one else saw you rushing home with grass and the morning dew all over your boots, Mr Brennan."

Alastair flinched and stood aside to let Gabriel in. "If anything happens, I shall deny that I was ever there," he hissed at Gabriel's back, a second before the monk whirled round like one of those slightly creepy magicians as they vanish into thin air in front of a stunned audience. Unfortunately for Alastair, Gabriel had not vanished and stood looking unblinking at him. "I didn't see *you*," Alastair added, folding his right arm across his body.

"Nobody ever sees what they do not expect to see," answered Gabriel, "and you were far too busy fleeing the scene of death, I think. Shall we sit down? I do not have long, but I have long enough to talk to you."

Alastair's shoulders drooped. He indicated the drawing room door and followed Gabriel inside. "I know how this looks," he began, then stopped, evidently sensing that he already sounded suspicious. "I had nothing to do with it, Father. I arrived within sight of the cottage to find the police already there. I knew I would find it hard to explain myself so I made myself scarce before anyone saw me. At least that was the plan."

Gabriel regarded the shabby brown sofa he had been about to sit on, thought better of it and perched on the wicker chair by the window. Like the Paiges' drawing room, there was an air of education and culture about the place, the presence of heaving bookshelves, a painting of a poppy made to look as though it had been magnified many times and then deliberately blurred. It was not to Gabriel's taste, but he suspected it would be the object Alastair would rescue if the house burnt down. On the other wall, there was a framed print of what appeared to be the front cover of a novel. A young girl, dressed in a crisp white summer dress, peered mournfully at him from beneath the words *Innocence Lost.*

Where this house differed from the other was the thinly disguised poverty written into the room. The furnishings were aged and threadbare; it was impossible not to notice the frayed edges of the hearth rug and the faded curtains that must have once been a rich red colour. Gabriel concentrated on the job at hand. "Do you often go out walking early in the morning, Mr Brennan?"

"Only when I can bring myself to," he answered, throwing himself down on the sofa and promptly sinking back several inches. "I'm a writer, Father. I feel most at peace in the hour after I wake up. A little like a monk, I suppose."

Gabriel blushed, thinking of the many times during the early months of his novitiate, when he had dragged himself out of bed in a thunderous temper. It had taken longer than he cared to admit to rejoice in the beauty of the early morning. "Do not take me as a model. You just happened to be out on a stroll and stumbled upon two bodies then?"

Alastair glared at him. "Look, I was miles away! That kid was screaming like a thing possessed! I heard him in the distance and went running to see if I could be of assistance. But as I said, I was a long way off, and by the time I got close to the cottage the police were already there. I could see one of them being as sick as a dog outside."

"That was not a policeman, it was Brother Gerard."

Alastair shrugged. "Oh, well all I saw was a little black figure."

Gabriel hesitated. "You still appear to have taken rather

a long time to get there—the same time it took for the boy to get to the abbey, make himself understood, and then Brother Gerard and I to make our way to the cottage and discover the bodies."

"Are you calling me a liar?" Alastair was on his feet, his flushed face turning a livid shade of purple. "You asked me a question, I have told you what happened. I heard screaming, hurried as quickly as I could in the direction of the cottage, realised something was up and legged it like the blazes. If you don't like my story, feel free to tell me another."

"I should like you to tell me another story," said Gabriel quietly, looking steadily down at his hands, "if you could bear it."

"There is no other story!"

"Not about this morning, Mr Brennan. I mean the story about the other time you fell under suspicion." He glanced up in time to see Alastair's glare give way to a look of bewilderment. "There was another time, wasn't there?"

"How the devil could you possibly know?" he asked, and he was almost pleading. "It was *years* ago, Father."

"Because I would like to believe that you are telling me the truth—though I fear that you are not telling me everything. And the only possible explanation for your behaviour this morning would be that you have fallen foul of the authorities before and naturally ran at the first sight of trouble."

Alastair looked fixedly at Gabriel as though trying to calculate whether his bluff was being called. "I hardly need to remind a priest that no one—including your good self—has a right to the truth."

"I'm afraid I am a Benedictine, not a Jesuit. Not sure

I entirely agree with you on that point anyhow." Gabriel noticed a rosewood cabinet in the corner, on which stood a number of crystal glasses. "Why not pour yourself a stiff drink? It's a little early but you've had a shock."

Alastair raised his hand in weary surrender and turned away. "Very well," he said, pulling a half-empty bottle from the cabinet, "if you're prepared to listen, which is more than what most people are prepared to do."

"Is your connection to Marie or to her husband?" Gabriel began. "You are close to both of them now, but the connection obviously runs deeper than that."

Alastair held the bottle between his legs to open it one-handed and filled a glass a little too full. "It is no secret that I am on very friendly terms with the Paiges. There's not much in the way of intelligent conversation to be had in a dump like this. They are educated, interesting people. Naturally I enjoy their society."

"When did you first meet her?" Alastair continued to stand as though he suspected he would have to make a run for it. Gabriel pointed in the direction of the poster. "Come now, Brennan, I am not a reader of novels but I can use my eyes. Is Marie your lost innocent?"

Alastair clutched the drink like a lifeline. "That's either an extraordinary hunch or you've been watching me, Father," he said quietly. "Is it truly so obvious?"

"No, not at all. I'm one of life's observers, that's all. It seems to me that you like her and the feeling—however chaste—runs quite deep. When did you first meet her?"

"I taught her, Father, when she was at school before the War." He took a long draught of the drink before turning to face the window. "Her mother was Belgian. She grew up in

Belgium, but her English father insisted that she be sent to a boarding school in England. I taught French and German. Not that I had much to teach her, she had an extraordinary gift for languages. Particularly French of course, it was her mother tongue."

"Indeed."

"I was very young, rather gauche if I'm honest, and I suppose I paid too much attention to her."

"You found her attractive?"

"Not like that, Father!" Alastair tapped his head against the window frame. "I swear I never touched her! Of course I liked her, it's impossible not to like a pupil who loves one's subject so much. And she was unhappy. She was often homesick, and she was painfully sensitive. I was . . . *drawn* to her, I suppose."

Gabriel stood up and moved a little closer to where Alastair was standing. "I'm listening," he said. "You were drawn to her, you cared about her. There's nothing wrong in that as such. What happened?"

"Nothing," hissed Alastair through his teeth. "Nothing on my part, I assure you. Some nasty, venomous little gossip told the headmistress a dirty tale about me. You hardly need me to elaborate, I suspect."

Gabriel groaned. He knew nothing about girls' boarding schools, but he knew enough about the claustrophobic, insular world of any institution to guess just how easy it would have been for such a rumour to spread. All the more so if it involved a handsome young man in an otherwise exclusively female environment and a girl who had perhaps provoked a certain amount of jealousy among her peers without meaning to. "And she was believed?"

"Naturally. The nasty little minx also happened to be Sister's little darling. Deputy head girl, no less. The headmistress had had her reservations about employing me in the first place, said I was too young and handsome to be let loose among three hundred girls. Sorry if that sounds conceited, Father, but it was what she said on my first day."

Gabriel nodded. "I can quite imagine. Were you arrested?"

"Yes. Got off with a scolding from some sergeant. Then I was flung out on my ear. Of course, I could never teach again." He took another swig of the drink, then another; Gabriel was beginning to regret suggesting it. Alastair obviously needed very little encouragement to reach for that cabinet. "I lived hand to mouth until war broke out and I could join up. I must have been one of the few people in the country who was relieved when it came."

"And Marie?"

"I heard nothing more of her until after she married Dickie. That was when I found out that she had been expelled and sent back to Belgium. The worst of it was that her father believed the rumours too and never forgave her. He refused to send her to another school. Her education ended, and then of course she was trapped in Belgium after the Germans invaded."

"I'm sorry." It sounded so lame, but it was all Gabriel could think of saying. "Poor girl."

"It's amazing how much harm one lie can do, isn't it?" said Alastair, turning to face Gabriel. His eyes were red, either from the drink or tears he was too proud to shed in front of another man. "If it hadn't been for that brat, Marie might have spent the War safely tucked away in an English convent school. Life would have turned out very differently for her."

"She has suffered?"

"Far more than you know—or even I know, I suspect. Excuse me." He turned abruptly back to the window. Gabriel heard the gasping, gulping noises of a man battling to hold himself together. "She said the worst part of it," Alastair resumed, "far worse than anything else that happened, was that her father never spoke to her again. He was killed shortly after Belgium fell, never having been reconciled with her. So yes, I did want to protect her, but she's the sort of woman who provokes those feelings in men. She has always seemed so delicate. But I have great admiration for Dickie too, and I wouldn't want to see harm come to either of them. They do not deserve this."

Gabriel stood up to leave. "I am so sorry to have put you through so much this morning, Mr Brennan. I will show myself out." He lingered at the door. "There is one last question I would like to ask, if I may? Do you know how to fire a gun?"

Alastair gave Gabriel a bitter smile. "Father, half the men in England know how to fire a gun. You know perfectly well that the British Army does not send men into battle without a little training. Before you try any harder to pin this on me, if I had wanted to kill that man, I would have aimed at his head to make absolutely sure I killed him. And I would never raise my hand against a woman, especially not Marie."

I am not sure you would, thought Gabriel, as he hurried in the direction of the hospital. *But you love her more than you will ever admit to anyone, and in a fit of jealous rage a man cannot be trusted. And I never said she was beaten; I never said where he was shot.*

6

Gabriel arrived at the hospital to find Dominic standing nervously outside the front entrance. "Oh there you are!" Dominic exclaimed, as soon as Gabriel came into sight. "Where on earth have you been?"

"Sorry, old man," ventured Gabriel, "I didn't think you would get here so quickly."

"I cadged a lift on the way. Cuthbert said it was urgent, he was terribly worried about you."

"He shouldn't be."

They stepped into the main corridor of the hospital, and Gabriel was immediately assaulted by the smell of disinfectant. "Cuthbert said something about the mortuary," said Dominic. "I assumed you wanted me to look at the body, so I asked permission to view it. No one seemed to mind."

"Did you? Gosh."

"No need to sound so surprised."

"Not at all," answered Gabriel, apologetically. Dominic had many talents, but the ability to use his initiative was not normally one of them; Gabriel was astonished that he had had the presence of mind to get on with things. "Well?"

"He was shot in the stomach."

"Yes I know that!" said Gabriel, a little too loudly. A

passing nurse scowled at him. "I could see that when I first found him."

"I say, you might be a little more appreciative. Father Abbot will take a very dim view of my dashing off like this, it's no easy business."

"I'm sorry." Gabriel found a small alcove and dragged Dominic into it so that they could talk a little more privately. "Go on."

"It was a single wound. Other than that, there was some grazing to his left cheek but that may have been caused by the fall. Also, he had a tattoo on his arm. About here." He drew an invisible line across his forearm. "A six-digit number."

"Did he indeed?" Gabriel leant back against the wall. "I think we had better find Marie."

Dominic struggled to keep up as Gabriel rushed down the corridor. "What are you expecting to find?"

"Nothing, my friend," he called back over his shoulder. "I never expect to find anything, but there is something I would be most interested to find."

The two men had a nasty encounter with a Presbyterian matron who would have been quite at home in Calvin's Geneva, but she was eventually prevailed upon to leave Marie's side so that they could anoint her. "You have five minutes," she said sharply, poking her plump, scrubbed face round the door as she left. "I will not leave her longer than that."

Marie looked remarkably serene, enveloped in the crisp white hospital sheets. Her normally anxious face was smooth and relaxed with the deep sleep of her coma, and if her head had not been so elaborately bandaged, she might have looked as though she were about to wake up and embrace the day. In her calm state, Gabriel was reminded of how young she was. Somehow, whenever he had seen her walking around or stopped to talk with her, he had found it impossible to place her age; he had always known her to talk and move like a much more mature woman, but she could not have been older than her mid-twenties.

"What a pity," said Dominic, who unlike Gabriel had noticed only what was wrong. "What a dreadful pity."

"What do you make of it?"

Dominic glanced at Marie's face. The bandaging was holding a thick dressing across one side of her head, down to just below her ear. Her lips were cracked and swollen, but besides that, her face had hardly been touched. The blood Gabriel remembered seeing all over her face had not been hers. Dominic reached for the notes clipped to the end of the metal-framed bed. "I'm not sure I should be doing this."

"Just get on with it!"

Gabriel's attention was drawn to Marie's left hand, which was tightly bandaged with her fourth and fifth fingers tied together and the thumb covered in thick padding. He leant across and pulled back the loose white sleeve of her hospital gown to reveal what he had suspected would be waiting for him—etched in black across the taut, pale flesh of her forearm was a six-digit serial number.

"You know, this doesn't tell you anything you did not already know," said Dominic, looking up from the notes without noticing what Gabriel was looking at. "Fractures, bruises, the broken fingers might be a sign she put up a struggle. Having said that, her hand may have been stamped on after she was knocked down."

"I'm afraid I can't quite imagine Marie putting up much resistance. She barely had the strength to climb the stairs."

"The blow to the head is the most serious injury. She's fortunate it didn't kill her outright." He stopped, hearing the regular rat-a-tat of shoes marching along the tiled corridor. He replaced the notes. "I'd look busy if I were you."

Gabriel threw himself onto his knees and clutched his hands in front of him, bowing his head and closing his eyes in a pose of fervent prayer. A moment later, the matron put her head round the door to see if they were finished, tutted quietly and walked away again. Gabriel looked up at Dominic. "That was remiss of me. I should have anointed her first. You'd better return to the abbey, I've put you to quite enough trouble as it is."

Dominic shook his head. "It's quite all right, old man; this is my morning for visiting the sick. And poor Mrs Paige may not require many more visits." He signalled for Gabriel to move away from Marie's bedside and stood as far from her as possible. "There's something you should know," he whispered. "I don't know much about murder, but there's something twisted about all this. She's so badly injured she may never regain consciousness, but her attacker has hardly touched her face. She has multiple fractures, extensive bruising, but I would at least expect her to have a black eye. There's something else." He paused to catch his breath. "Pederson was not shot cleanly at all. He could have been shot through the head or the heart and died instantly, but this was a slow, painful death. I can't help thinking that whoever pulled the trigger meant him to suffer. Either that or the murderer meant him to witness Marie's execution shortly before he himself died."

Gabriel sank into silence while he considered what had been said. "Will she live?"

"I wouldn't get your hopes up on that score, I'm afraid. A strong, healthy man would be in with a halfway decent chance, but she was weak to begin with. Even if she does recover, it is very likely that she will remember nothing of what happened. "

Gabriel murmured his thanks and waited until Dominic had left before attending to Marie. It served the purpose of reminding him that, first and foremost, he was a priest, and he forced himself to stop thinking about all the unanswered questions as he dipped his thumb into the oil and traced the Sign of the Cross over her closed eyes, the dressing covering her damaged ear, her bloodied lips. *Per istam Sanctam unctionem et suam Piissimam misericordiam, indulgeat tibi Dominus quidquid deliquisti.*

As Gabriel turned Marie's undamaged hand over, he had another surprise. Across the palm there was a jagged scar, which ran across the centre of her hand like a piece of barbed wire. He felt a pulse racing in his neck. A terrible thought struck him, so obvious he could not believe it had never occurred to him before.

~

"Dr Paige, you are not making your case any easier by refusing to cooperate with me," said Inspector Applegate, glowering at his suspect across the table. The two men had been seated in the interview room for over an hour, and Applegate felt hot and restless. He had not expected a character like Dr Paige to be an easy subject, but the man seemed determined to do everything possible to antagonise him. They were off to a very bad start indeed when Applegate lit a cigarette and Dr Paige broke his silence only to demand that he put it out. When Applegate refused, partly because he desperately needed a cigarette and partly because he wanted to retrieve some control over the situation, Paige refused to speak at all until the inspector obediently stubbed the wretched thing out in the ashtray.

"What has happened to my wife?" asked Dr Paige for the umpteenth time. "My place is at her side."

"Your wife is alive and is being perfectly well cared for at the hospital," replied Applegate yet again, "and I'll be the judge of where you need to be. For the time being I need you to stay here and answer some questions. Now, about the bruises Mrs Webb found on your wife's arm. Can you explain—"

"I have already explained that she got those bruises from iron injections," Dr Paige responded, enunciating every word as though talking to a first-year medical student. "My wife is anaemic. I was as careful as I could be, but unfortunately iron injections tend to cause bruising."

"Is it normal for a doctor to give injections to members of his own family?"

"I'll say this one more time. Many doctors treat their own family. As a matter of fact, I would have preferred her to go to the hospital, but she's afraid of needles and she's afraid of hospitals. So I gave them to her myself."

"A doctor seems an odd choice of husband for a woman with those kinds of fears, wouldn't you say?"

Dr Paige drummed his knuckles against the edge of the table. "I am not in the habit of walking around my house in my white coat, waving hypodermic needles in her face. We doctors look quite like normal people in the comfort of our own homes."

Applegate continued to look steadily at him, encouraged by the creeping sense of panic in the doctor's voice. "I'm very glad to hear it, Doctor."

"Do I really look like a wife-beater to you?"

"If you can tell me what a wife-beater looks like, I may be able to give you an answer."

"I'm a doctor!" shouted Dr Paige, abandoning all pretence of poise. "You have heard the words 'first do no harm' I suppose?"

Applegate feigned confusion. "Well, I'm sure it's very likely that no doctor has ever hit a woman in the whole of human history, no doctor has ever murdered his wife and her lover in a fit of jealous rage—"

"She was not having an affair!"

Applegate watched Dr Paige cover his face, waiting until he was absolutely sure the man would not shout again. "Then please explain the note we found in your jacket."

"I—I can't explain it," he almost whispered, "I don't understand it. I can't read German." He lifted his head to look at Applegate and looked suddenly desperate, as though the seriousness of the situation were finally dawning on him. "This is going to sound most unlikely to you, but when I found that note, I was sure she had left it for me to find. Perhaps she had forgotten that I don't understand German or thought I would understand the significance of it regardless. I just knew she was in danger and I went out to look for her."

Applegate dropped the note on the desk, equidistant

between them. It was written on crumpled white paper that looked as though it had been torn out of a notebook. Applegate did not understand the brief message scrawled untidily across the paper either, but they could both see the initial "M" at the top and a florid "J" signing the missive off. "Imagine yourself in court, Dr Paige," suggested Applegate calmly. "A woman is found virtually in the arms of a man to whom she is not married. He's dead; she's been left for dead. Her husband is found in the vicinity in an excitable state with what looks like a love letter in his possession. A jury might conclude that you caught them in the act, shot your rival and turned your rage against your wife."

"You disgust me."

"A pity you feel that way, Dr Paige." Applegate leant forwards, elbows on the table, chin resting lightly on his hands. "Not very hard for me to build a case against you, is it, Doctor?"

Dr Paige was beginning to sweat, mostly due to the heat of a windowless room in the middle of summer, but Applegate saw only fear. "I have no idea what that letter says," repeated the doctor. "Neither do you."

"That doesn't matter. It looks like a love letter, you could be forgiven for thinking it was. And the fact that she went to him after reading it rather suggests it was, doesn't it?"

Applegate would never quite forgive Gabriel for wrecking the tension he had succeeded in creating by bursting in at that precise moment, red-faced, breathless and sweating profusely. "Inspector!" he puffed, leaning on the doorframe for support, "Inspector Applegate, I'm so sorry but I must speak with you immediately!" He glanced over Applegate's shoulder at Dr Paige, who was looking pale and steely, but not a little relieved by the intrusion. "Dr Paige, I'm so sorry. I have been to visit Mrs Paige—"

Dr Paige jumped to his feet. "Well? Is she conscious? Is she awake?"

Applegate stepped between them as though the two men had been about to start a fist fight. He took a step in Gabriel's direction, followed by another so that Gabriel had no choice but to scramble backwards out of the room or risk being trampled on. "What do you think you're doing?" he hissed, letting the door slam behind him. "What do you think this is, a circus?"

"Inspector, forgive me, but I think you must send a constable to guard Mrs Paige's bedside."

"I beg your pardon?" Whatever Applegate had expected Gabriel to say, it was not this and he was thrown off guard. "What are you talking about?"

"It occurred to me when I was at the hospital—"

"What were you doing at the hospital?"

"Administering the last rites to a gravely ill Catholic," he answered, stung by the accusatory tone, "and minding my own business. She was supposed to die this morning. The killer left her for dead. When word gets out that she is alive, he may have another try."

Applegate narrowed his eyes. "I hardly think that will be necessary, Father," he said. "I'm about to charge Dr Paige with murder and attempted murder. I think she'll be safe enough, assuming she can cling onto life."

Gabriel bowed his head. "You know, he may not have done it. Or at least he may not have acted alone."

Applegate turned his back on Gabriel and busied himself opening the door he had so recently slammed in Dr Paige's face. "Thank you for your contribution, Father. If you hadn't come barging in like that I would have had a confession out of him by now."

Gabriel shuffled his feet against the tiled floor. "I wonder if I might talk to him, Inspector? I'm quite keen on confession too."

"You've a blasted nerve asking me for anything."

"I know, old chap," he answered cheerfully. "I've been told that once or twice before. And I really would send someone to guard Mrs—"

"You can have five minutes if you get off my back for the rest of the investigation."

"But of course, Inspector."

It was not a lie, thought Gabriel, as he was ushered in to see Dr Paige. He had no intention of climbing on top of Inspector Applegate's back; the strain would probably kill him at his age.

7

"Don't try anything," snarled Dr Paige as Gabriel closed the door behind him, signalling to Applegate that he wished him to stay outside. "If you've come to blackmail me into making a confession, you can leave now."

Gabriel pulled Applegate's recently vacated chair away from the table and sat down. He noticed that Dr Paige had abandoned his seat altogether and was standing in the farthest corner of the room with his back pressing against the wall as though he anticipated a fight. "I have anointed your wife. I thought it was what she would have wanted."

Dr Paige nodded, relaxing just a little. "Thank you. She would have called for a priest if she could. Is there any sign of improvement?"

"It's a little soon," said Gabriel gently. "Don't lose hope."

"She was not in a state of mortal sin, Father," he added. "I know there are some dreadful things being said of her but she was not that sort of woman. I ought to know."

"She seemed to me to be a good woman. I should have liked to have known her better."

The doctor's brows furrowed. "Would you mind awfully not referring to her in the past tense, Father? She's not dead."

"Forgive me, a slip of the tongue. Why don't you sit down?"

Paige shook his head. "I'll stand if you don't mind, Father. This room gives me the creeps. That inspector's more or less tied the rope around my neck already."

"Where did you meet her? Marie, I mean."

Paige looked askance at him. He tried to think of a reason the question might be a trap but could not think of one. "Belsen, as it happens."

"The concentration camp?"

"The very same. Unless you know of another Belsen I've never had the pleasure of visiting." He shook his head. "I'm so sorry, Father, I don't mean to sound so aggressive. It's just a little hard to speak about, even now."

"I understand."

"No you don't!" he snapped, making Gabriel jump. "Everyone says that and they haven't a clue!"

"Sorry, I didn't mean it like that."

"I don't care what you meant. I'm a grown man and I will not break down in front of you."

An unpleasant silence descended between them. Gabriel was aware that Applegate might burst in at any moment and there might not be another chance for them to speak, but he also knew he had made a disastrous start and needed time to make amends. "If it helps," he began cautiously, "when I saw Dimbleby's film, I wept like a baby. I'm sure I was not the only grown man to do so. If you were there, I think you may behave as you wish."

"Those pictures showed you nothing," said Dr Paige quietly, looking away. "Pictures never do, even good ones. They did not convey the silence . . . or the stench. There were hardened soldiers on their hands and knees vomiting, there were men in tears. I went into a hut full of bodies. Row upon row in wooden bunks. Most of them dead, a few groaning and struggling to move—they mostly died later. That was when I saw her."

"Marie was a prisoner?"

But Dr Paige was speaking as though in a trance and did not hear the interruption. "She was curled up in a corner as though she had fallen where she stood, too exhausted to move another step. I went to press my fingers against her neck to check her pulse and she grabbed my wrist. I actually screamed and tried to run, but she wouldn't let go. She was like a corpse coming to life. I could not believe how strong she was. She's not as frail as she looks."

"I can imagine." Across the table in Dr Paige's direction Gabriel surreptitiously pushed a clean handkerchief, which the doctor took automatically.

"She said, 'Help me', in English, as clear as a bell. Then she looked at me and said, 'Help me or shoot me dead now. You will not leave me here.' So I wrapped her in my jacket and carried her out."

"That's extraordinary. You must be—you must be very proud of her."

"Oh yes." Dr Paige had slipped out of his trance and was looking intently at Gabriel as though making absolutely sure he had his full attention. "You see, Father, she never had to find herself in such a place. She could have kept her head down and got herself through the War in one piece. I suspect it's what I would have done given half a chance, but she didn't."

"Resistance?"

"She was a courier. She was captured on her eighteenth birthday, betrayed to the Gestapo by a girl she believed to be her closest friend."

A thick, ominous hush crept over the room, and this time Gabriel was not sure how to break it. He wished he had probed Marie's past a little further with Alastair to avoid making her husband rake over it. "I'm sorry."

"I know how this looks," said Dr Paige finally, "but you must understand I could never hurt her. I never found out what her dealings were with Johannes Pederson, but whatever it was, she wanted me to know what was going on."

"Have you any idea?"

Dr Paige shook his head wearily. "There were many closed doors in Marie's life. There is a great deal she has never told me, and I have not wanted to intrude too far. I do not know everything the Gestapo did to her—I can guess, of course, but she has never been specific. I don't know everything that happened to her in the camps. Pederson was Danish. Perhaps he was in the resistance too?"

"I was told he was a war hero."

"Perhaps they were both being hunted down, and he was trying to warn her. There are still Nazis at large, so many of them escaped justice." He started suddenly. "Father, is Marie's life still in danger? I mean from the killer, I thought I heard you say—"

"I have asked Inspector Applegate to send a constable to the hospital. I am not sure if the killer will risk entering the hospital and making another attempt on her life, and he may not be aware yet that she survived the attack. I merely thought it prudent."

The door handle rattled. "Father, I cannot bear the irony

74

of a woman surviving the Gestapo and the SS and dying in this tiny village under my very nose." The door swung open. "Help me," he whispered.

Applegate stood in the doorway looking at them. "Time's up, gentlemen."

~

Gabriel's sense of timing had never been as keen as he should have liked, but even he had to admit he had made a particularly awful mess of the situation as he hurried from the abbot's room as fast as his legs could carry him. It was not just that he had meant to apologise for being away so long and had somehow forgotten to say the word "sorry", it was that Gabriel had asked a question he had really had no right to ask at any time, let alone then.

Gabriel knew that Abbot Ambrose had had a shadowy war, which he was not permitted to talk about to anyone. Frankly, this was hardly a problem as Abbot Ambrose was not a man to indulge in intimate conversation at the best of times, but he had always made it quite clear that he had no desire whatsoever to talk about those years. It had never occurred to Gabriel to be nosy, but he had never needed information so urgently before. In the end, he had not been able to think of an easy way to ask the question that had been going round his head all through lunch, and in the absence of an alternative, Gabriel had introduced the subject as directly as he could. "Father Abbot, when you, erm, *travelled* during the War, did you ever come across the concentration camps?"

Not what Mr Churchill would have called his finest hour.

All in all, Gabriel could not help feeling he had asked to find himself standing in the empty corridor with the sound of the slamming door ringing in his ears. He looked about him, grateful that no one appeared to have witnessed the scene, and pondered his next move. He had also meant to ask the abbot's permission to investigate further. Now that he thought about it, he should have asked that question first, but he did not dare knock on the door again in case Abbot Ambrose hurled him out the window instead of the door this time. He had been angry enough for anything.

The door flew open, as aggressively as it had so recently been slammed, causing Gabriel to stagger back. Abbot Ambrose stood in the doorway, but instead of being red-faced and furious, he looked solemn and a little ashamed. "Come in," he said tonelessly.

Gabriel faltered before following Abbot Ambrose inside. As soon as the door had closed again, Ambrose began talking a little too quickly as though desperate to get the conversation over with. "Forgive me, Gabriel, I had no business turning on you like that. I'm afraid I was a little taken aback, you bringing up the subject out of the blue."

"No, I'm the one who should be sorry," said Gabriel, waiting while Ambrose settled himself back into his chair before sitting down himself. "I could not think of an easy way to ask."

"I can think of quite a few ways you might have asked," Abbot Ambrose retorted. "You might start by telling me why you suddenly wish to know? A little context helps a fellow enormously."

"Yes of course. I went to anoint Mrs Paige this morning."

Abbot Ambrose rolled his eyes. "I suspect you did one or two other things on your way, but we'll let that pass for the minute, shall we?"

Gabriel was delighted to let it pass. "I noticed that she had a number tattooed onto her arm," he said. "So did the dead man."

Abbot Ambrose flinched. "I see."

"Dr Paige said that Marie had been in Belsen concentration camp."

Abbot Ambrose shook his head. "No, if she had a tattoo she was in Auschwitz." He noted Gabriel's confusion. "The Nazis used a number of means of identifying prisoners —numbers, badges, symbols. But these things were usually sewn onto uniforms. They only used tattoos in Auschwitz."

"Dr Paige definitely said she was in Belsen. He was part of the liberation."

Ambrose considered the matter. "It's not impossible that she ended up there. And this other chap perhaps, God rest his soul. Prisoners were moved around. But at some point they must both have been in Auschwitz."

"Could they have met there? It's just that they obviously knew one another, either from the War or perhaps before that, but it's hard to see how two people from different countries could have been thrown together before the War."

Ambrose shook his head. "The fact that they were both prisoners may be a coincidence. There were so many thousands of them."

"A huge coincidence under the circumstances." Gabriel would not normally have argued with Abbot Ambrose about anything, but for the moment they felt like equals working out a puzzle together. "Two survivors of the concentration camps meet in a sleepy English village. Both are attacked at the same time, in the same place . . ."

"Gabriel, I hardly need you to state the obvious," Ambrose answered, showing the telltale signs of temper creeping up on him. "When people arrived at the camps, the men and women were separated. As far as I am aware, this was the case in all of the camps. They would not have met. If they were acquainted with one another, it was before or after the War."

Gabriel rubbed his temples. "Oh dear, I have more questions now than I began with!"

Abbot Ambrose smiled. "That may not be such a bad sign. But I'm afraid I have not been of much assistance, have I?"

"No, no, there's little point in my barking up the wrong tree." He had to ask the question. "Father Abbot, please let me investigate this matter a little further." He waited for a response but Ambrose was silent. He plucked up the courage to continue: "Dr Paige has been charged with Pederson's murder and his wife's attempted murder. If she dies —and she may—he will be put on trial for two murders I do not believe he committed."

"Gabriel, do not be misguided by your own innocence. If you think him incapable of such a crime, you may think again."

Gabriel shook his head. "Perhaps not incapable but there are other possibilities. And Applegate has practically summoned the hangman. Paige has asked me to help him."

"Has he indeed? Did they release him from custody so that he could attend to the wife they think he tried to murder?"

Gabriel could not meet Abbot Ambrose's eye. "I only

went to the police station after I had anointed Marie. It dawned on me that she might need protection." He braced himself for a rebuke but none came. "Please."

Ambrose looked down at the edge of the desk for an inordinately long time; never a good sign. "These are very deep waters, Gabriel. I have seen good men go to their deaths before because they misjudged the strength of the enemy or failed to recognise the enemy until it was too late."

"I am not in danger."

"You may well be. You've no idea what it was like in those places, very few do."

"That's exactly what Dr Paige said," Gabriel put in, then regretted the interruption. "Forgive me."

"If our two victims survived Hitler's camps," Ambrose continued as though Gabriel had not spoken, "they did so by cheating death every single day. Then they come to a country of safety, one of them ends up dead, the other is at death's door. Whoever did this was absolutely determined to silence them where other evil men had already failed. And whoever it was might not take kindly to interference."

Gabriel opened his mouth to tell Ambrose about Dominic's comments on the cruelty of the murder, but remembered himself just in time. "There was something else. I presume you read German?"

"If absolutely necessary, yes."

Gabriel held out a folded piece of paper, torn from a notebook. "Please could you tell me what this says?"

Ambrose looked at the missive with evident distaste. "Where did you find this?"

"Dr Paige was found with a note in his pocket, written by Pederson to Marie. I made a copy when—"

Ambrose snatched the paper from him. "If that ghastly inspector comes for you, I shall deny any knowledge of your activities." Ambrose looked back at the page. "Is this exactly what was written in the original note?"

"Yes, Father Abbot. I copied it as I found it—I do not understand German. Dr Paige said he didn't either."

Ambrose handed back the paper. "I'm sorry, Gabriel, but I'm afraid this will not help your friend in the least."

"What does it say?"

"It is obviously a love letter. 'Do not make me search for you among the crowds. Come quickly to me this time, little one.' All that sort of gibberish."

Gabriel could not hide his disappointment. "I see."

"If anything, Dr Paige has damned himself by being found with a note like that in his pocket. Everything points in his direction."

8

"You know, it would help if you gave me a hint," suggested Gerard, looking at Gabriel for a prompt. "This place gives me the heebie-jeebies."

Gabriel stood in the middle of Pederson's cottage, silently taking in the details of the room again. The absence of the bodies made the room just about bearable to enter; but it had still not been cleaned up, and the blood splashed across the floor left the air heavy with the smell of death. "Just be quiet and look."

"I haven't an earthly clue what I'm supposed to be seeing! You know, I can smell rotting flesh. I reckon some tiny bits of him ended up in the corners when they shot him."

"If you feel sick, get a breath of fresh air," said Gabriel without looking at him. "I don't think it smells too bad under the circumstances. Just a minute—why did you say 'they'?"

Gerard made for the door. "Because if Dr Paige didn't do it—and you're desperate for him not to have done it—it was obviously more than one person, wasn't it?"

Gabriel watched Gerard's short figure through the open doorway as he hunched up retching. "I'm sorry, I should never have brought you here again. I thought something might jog your memory." He stepped out and patted Gerard on the shoulder. "Go back to the abbey, it's all right."

Gerard stood up, gasping for breath. "What are you trying to find?"

Gabriel shrugged. "I'm not sure I know. Something feels so wrong about this room and I have no idea why."

"It looks exactly as an artist's place ought to look," Gerard returned, "down to the tiniest detail. Apart from the blood sloshing about, of course, but you know what I mean. There is nothing wrong."

"That's just it," Gabriel persisted, "it feels impeccably correct down to the tiniest detail. Which is so wrong."

Gerard rolled his eyes. "Why?"

"I mean it's not idiosyncratic enough somehow," Gabriel explained. "It feels like the sort of room a person would have if he wanted everyone to believe he was an artist."

"Gabriel, he *was* an artist," corrected Gerard. "I saw him out painting. Sat there for hours with his easel and box of paints and brushes and the like. I watched him painting. No mystery there."

Gabriel twisted his heels into the floor in irritation. "All right, he may well have been an artist but it still feels fake. His whole identity feels fake. The man claims to be Danish, but he's heard speaking German, he writes a note in German. If you were a German wanting to live quietly, wouldn't you pretend to be Scandinavian? One could be pretty sure the average Englishman wouldn't notice the difference."

"Gordon Merriott said he heard him speaking German, that's not quite the same thing as him actually speaking it, is it? He said Marie Paige was speaking German as well, for that matter, and she's obviously not German herself."

Gabriel looked intently around the room. It was very close to how he remembered it, though in the panic of finding the bodies that morning he had not had much of a chance to take in the details. His eyes rested on a painted canvas pinned against the far wall. It looked as though it had been rolled up for a time, for the bottom curled slightly upwards. "That's curious."

Gerard followed his gaze. "Never liked modern art me-self," said Gerard. "A five-year-old could do that and get it hung up in some gallery."

"You sound like an old man." He had a point but the painting, though abstract, was skilfully wrought. A female figure jumped out of the picture in swirls of livid red with a few shades of charcoal here and there to add detail. The woman looked as though she were turning around to face the viewer, and she appeared to be wearing a veil or head covering of some kind, which gave her a Madonna-like qual-ity. Red not blue, but then Gabriel wondered whether he would instinctively see the Virgin Mary when he saw any veiled woman. It might not have been deliberate.

"There's nothing wrong with a person wanting to hide his past," Gerard persisted. "How would you like spending your life with little kids chanting *Heil Hitler* at you? You'd probably pretend you were something else."

"Are you playing devil's advocate or do you believe that?"

Gerard feigned surprise. "I thought I was here to chal-lenge your mad theories?"

"Does this all sound mad to you?"

"All right, not mad," said Gerard, "how about clutching at straws?"

Gabriel grimaced and turned his back, more out of the

desire to shut out a nuisance than the urge to sulk, which was precisely how it looked. "If I don't clutch at straws, no one else will."

Gerard went into conciliatory mode. "We're on the same side. I think. Listen, plenty of people on the Continent speak German, whether they like it or not. I'm just saying it might be the only language they shared. This is all strange enough without making mysteries where there are none."

"Yes, yes, yes, thank you very much," Gabriel retorted. "That's very helpful."

Gerard gave up. "Sorry, but you dragged me to this dump . . . oh, please excuse me—"

"Don't touch the window! Go outside if you feel sick," ordered Gabriel, watching as Gerard turned to the window with the obvious intention of letting in some air. "We're not supposed to touch anything."

Gerard pushed open the window with very little effort. "It wasn't shut," he said by way of justification. "The latch was hanging open. Well, it is summer, after all."

Gabriel joined Gerard at the window; the white paint coating the wooden window frame was peeled and grimy with age and probably the artist's poor housekeeping. Around the latch, there were fresh scratch marks where someone had battled to force the window open on a previous occasion, either because the latch had rusted and stiffened over time or because it had been forced open. "I'm going to clutch at straws again, if it's all the same to you," declared Gabriel, leaning out the window and immediately finding himself staring into a dank, thickly overgrown patch of greenery. "I might even risk being accused of making mysteries where there are none."

"Why don't you forget I ever said it?"

"Gerard, do me a favour and run round to the outside of this window, would you?"

Gerard groaned but did as he was told. If nothing else he could at least get out of the oppressive room. He appeared, seconds later, swallowing hard. "There's something—I've stubbed my toe on a stone."

"I knew you'd do that," said Gabriel with a satisfied smile. "Bend down and pick up the stone, there's a good chap. Wouldn't want anyone else bashing it."

Gerard muttered under his breath, threw himself down onto his hands and knees and placed his hands exactly where he thought he had been standing when he had hurt himself. He froze. "Let's get away from here," he whispered without looking up. "Now."

"Don't panic, Gerard. Pick it up."

"Holy Mother!"

"Quickly! Remove your jacket and use it to pick it up. Keep your fingerprints off it."

Too shocked to do anything but obey, Gerard picked up the offending object and dropped the bundle of his jacket into Gabriel's hands. "How did you know it was there? The police have already found the weapon."

Gabriel stepped into the sunlight and examined the muddy, blood-coated gun quickly before wrapping it up again.

"Well?" demanded Gerard.

"It occurred to me that if there were more than one murderer, there might be more than one weapon. When I saw that the window had recently been opened, clumsily, violently, I concluded that the other weapon must have been disposed of that way."

"But two guns? Only one of them was shot. Marie was —"

Gabriel stopped abruptly, looking round to ensure that they were not being overheard. "Another thing occurred to me in that room. What if—against all my instincts— Pederson and Mrs Paige had been involved in some sort of affair? We know very little about Marie Paige; even her husband knows precious little about the reasons for her imprisonment other than that she was in the resistance. If she were captured by the Gestapo, she may have been tortured."

"She most certainly was."

"Now, why are people put to torture?"

"Because—because someone wants to get a confession out of them or . . . or information, I suppose. What other reason would there be?"

"Precisely. And what if Marie Paige still had information? Something so important that a person might be prepared to pursue her all the way to England? Pederson could very easily have been used as a pawn to drag Marie into a deserted place. If they had intended to kill her, it would only have been after she had told them what they wanted."

"And Pederson?"

"Once he had served his purpose, he would have become an inconvenience."

Gerard ran his fingers through his hair. "It all sounds a bit *Boy's Own* to me. How on earth did the police miss that gun? It was hidden but not that well hidden."

"It may have been dropped there at a later hour, though I fail to see a reason why it would have been. I suspect it was simply that the police were not expecting to find it. Therefore they did not find it. People have a habit of missing what they do not expect to see. They had already found what they thought was the only weapon."

~

"It can't have been there when my men searched the vicinity," Applegate insisted, when the two monks appeared in his office brandishing a British service revolver. "They would never have missed that."

"If you say so, Inspector," Gabriel replied. "I think this may be the gun that was used to shoot Johannes Pederson."

Applegate opened up a clean handkerchief and took the weapon from Gabriel. "We already have a murder weapon; we lifted one gun from the scene immediately after the bodies were found. Heaven knows what this is all about."

"I wonder if I might have a look at that gun, Inspector? I mean, the gun you found? I have a little theory I should like to explore."

Applegate put the newly acquired piece of evidence on the desk between them. "Really? And I have a little murder case I should like to solve." Gabriel bristled at Applegate's affectation of his RP accent. He was sure he did not sound so posh. "Thank you for doing your civic duty and handing in this vital piece of evidence. Now, perhaps you would like to leave."

Gerard turned to go, then noticed Gabriel refusing to budge and stopped in solidarity. "Come on now, Inspector," said Gabriel. "It'll only take a moment, and you won't understand the true significance of that find if you simply file it away."

Applegate gave Gabriel a death stare, which he returned

with a disarming smile. "I have no intention of filing any-thing away." Gerard took a step back, but Gabriel was still not making any sign that he intended to move. "You're not going to leave me alone, are you?" asked Applegate, brush-ing past them on his way out of the room. "Do not touch that weapon until I come back."

Minutes later, he returned with a box containing the other gun. "Unfortunately, the weapon was so drenched in blood we didn't have much luck with fingerprints, and I suspect we won't find much on this other one if it's been stuck in damp grass. D'you gentlemen know much about guns, then?"

"As much as the next bloke," Gerard put in. "I was called up same as anybody else."

"For about five minutes."

"That gun's British, and that's German, for a start," Ger-ard said, ignoring the comment, "but then there are plenty of both kicking about the country, I dare say. You going to open them up? I don't want to get my grubby fingers all over them."

Applegate opened the chamber of the recently found British gun. "That's been fired," said Gerard, "and it was well looked after before it was dumped. Look at it. Was just the one bullet fired?"

"It would appear so. They found the bullet that went through Pederson but nothing else. The paper boy only heard the one shot."

"In that case, the gun you picked up was obviously never fired. You must've known there was another gun to be found."

Applegate's temper flared. "As a matter of fact I have been

88

a bit too busy interviewing our chief suspect to play little guessing games.''

"Are you absolutely certain, Gerard?" asked Gabriel, whose own knowledge of weaponry was rather more basic. "This is important."

"That German gun was never fired," he repeated. "It was never loaded. Look at it, the barrel's almost seized up." Gerard looked from Gabriel to Applegate and back again for an answer but neither man obliged. "Well?"

"You know something, Fr Gabriel?" said Applegate, as he carefully removed the evidence from his desk. He stoically ignored Gerard. "I would very much appreciate it if you could start coming up with some answers instead of giving me more and more questions."

"It does rather suggest that Dr Paige is innocent," Gabriel put in.

"No it don't, nothing like it. I'd hazard a guess that gun belonged to him. The German gun might have been Pederson's. Pederson would've known it wasn't loaded but tried to use it to scare off his attacker. There," he added, like a magician revealing the ace of spades. "Anything you'd like to add to that?"

~

"I wish we could have thought of something to add," lamented Gerard as they made their way back to the abbey.

"There was one thing, but I'm not sure the good inspector wishes to hear any more of my theories for today." Gabriel stopped walking. "Go back to the abbey now, Gerard. I need to return to the police station alone."

Gerard looked at his friend as though he were the biggest idiot in the country. "I thought you said—"

"Not to speak to Applegate. I need to speak to his suspect. The only thing I needed to add was that I'm not sure we are looking at a murder any longer. I'm not convinced we ever were."

9

Inspector Applegate could have awarded Gabriel full marks for cheek when he turned up at his office less than ten minutes after leaving. "What do you want?" he asked, before Gabriel could make any kind of explanation. "I'm warning you, Father, don't try my patience. I'm not sure why I'm humouring you at all really, but there we are."

"Most gracious of you," answered Gabriel. "I'm not here to be a pest as it happens, I think I might be able to help you this time."

Applegate raised an eyebrow. "And pigs might fly."

"I suppose they might," said Gabriel, matter-of-factly. "All things are possible."

"What do you want?"

"I need to talk to Dr Paige again."

"Out of the question. You've already spoken to him."

"I want to try to persuade him to confess."

Applegate started violently. "What?"

"Yes, and I think it might come better from me perhaps than from you, if you'll forgive me saying so."

"I'll forgive anything if you can wring a confession out of him."

"Wringing will not be necessary, Inspector. May I?"

Gabriel found Dr Paige sitting on his bed, leafing absently through a book someone had brought him. He looked up as soon as he heard the clank of the cell door heaving open. "Father I'm so glad to see you!" he cried, jumping to his feet. "Those idiots have charged me!"

"I know," said Gabriel, shaking Dr Paige's hand, "the Inspector told me."

"How is Marie? Is there any news of her?"

"None yet, I'm afraid. But no bad news either."

"Have you found anything? Anything at all that might help me?" Dr Paige was talking with the chaotic urgency of a man being driven slowly out of his mind by incarceration. He remained standing, ostensibly to offer Gabriel a place to sit, but rather than sitting down on the floor, Dr Paige stood with his back against the wall, clasping and unclasping his hands. "Well?"

"Brother Gerard found a British service revolver at the scene of the crime. It had been thrown out the window and since another gun was found at the scene, the police were not looking for it. Would it be yours, Dr Paige?"

Gabriel had noticed, as soon as he had entered the cell, that Dr Paige bore the look of a man on the brink of giving up—his face was haggard and unshaven when he would normally have been painstakingly fastidious, and he seemed maddeningly unable to stop fidgeting. At Gabriel's question he sank down onto the floor and appeared to start struggling for breath. "Oh God, I knew it!"

"Dr Paige—"

"I'm going to hang. Oh God—sorry Father, but—oh *God!*"

"Had you noticed that it was missing?"

"Yes, yes I had, the morning Marie was attacked. I always—I kept it in the same place, you see, and I saw that it was missing. I think I searched for it. But then with all the drama afterwards I never thought to mention it. Well, the gun they found was not that one, so I thought it must have been a coincidence that it was stolen. I couldn't even be sure when it had gone."

"How could you have known that they had found a different gun?"

"I . . ." Dr Paige floundered helplessly. "I'm sure I heard someone say something . . . or perhaps I even saw it. I honestly can't remember. I was worrying about my wife for goodness sake!"

"You told yourself it was not your gun. You wanted it to be a coincidence."

Dr Paige squeezed his hands together until they started to tremble with the effort. "For pity's sake, I wanted it to be! I have to get out of here."

"I might be able to help you with that," said Gabriel softly, "if you are prepared to cooperate with me."

"Of course I'll cooperate, what do you want? What else do I need to tell you?"

Gabriel swallowed. "Are you absolutely certain that your wife was not having an affair with Johannes Pederson?"

Dr Paige slammed his head back against the wall. "For God's sake, Father!"

"I have to ask."

Dr Paige stood up, staggering slightly with the sudden drop in blood pressure. "You need do no such thing. I have already told you she was not having an affair. It's a disgusting suggestion. If you were not a man of the cloth I'd break your nose!"

"I am sure you are capable of doing far worse."

Paige looked down at his clenched fists. "I could say I was provoked."

"You could say you were provoked in that cottage."

Paige let his hands hang limply by his sides. "Look, Father," he said, "the first time I set eyes on my wife, she was emaciated, filthy and infested with lice. If you think my love was a passing fancy, I beg you to reconsider."

Gabriel looked fixedly at the floor, feeling the heat of Dr Paige's anger filling the small room. "I do not doubt the depth of your love for your wife, Dr Paige," he said, hesitantly, "but is there not a chance that she felt differently?"

Dr Paige turned his back. Gabriel knew the man would have stormed out of the room if he had been at liberty to do so—or possibly given him an almighty punch on the nose, whatever the risk of excommunication—but he settled for the next best option and glowered at the wall. "You know nothing about love, Father, or marriage. I suppose I should forgive you for being so shallow."

Gabriel brushed off the insult. "Did Johannes threaten you when you confronted him at the cottage? If you shot him after he had pointed a gun at you and you had every reason to believe he would pull the trigger, it would be self-defence not murder. And if Marie lives—and God willing she will—your charge will be grievous bodily harm. You will not hang for that."

Paige refused to turn round. "I'm not sure what sort of a man you take me for," he said finally, "but I will not confess to a crime I did not commit because you have found a way to save me from the hangman. What happened in that cottage was murder and attempted murder. Deep down, I think you know that. And I didn't do it."

"Dr Paige, the letter—"

"She was a clever woman, Father. If she had been having an affair, she would have found some way to keep it hidden from me. God knows she keeps enough things secret. She wanted me to find that letter. There was something she wanted me to do, but she overestimated my own intelligence, I'm afraid. Or so it would appear."

"Have you—"

"Leave me alone. I'm sorry I ever asked for your help."

The man is either wholly innocent or wholly arrogant, thought Gabriel, shaking his head in Applegate's direction as he left to indicate that his plan had been unsuccessful. *He either persists in his claim that he is innocent because he truly is innocent and believes that justice will prevail, or he sincerely believes he has the power to persuade a jury to acquit him when the case against him is so childishly simple.*

Dr Paige's rebuff had been predictable enough, but Gabriel was more worldly-wise than anyone—with the possible exception of Abbot Ambrose—would ever suspect. He knew all too well that a woman might tire of the relentless attention of a man prone to being a little overbearing, a little too protective, and find herself searching for ways to spread her wings. Particularly a woman like Marie, who had spent years fending for herself under the most dangerous of circumstances and might no longer desire to have a saviour watching her every move now that her strength was returning. But Gabriel could also imagine the sense of betrayal a man like Dr Paige might feel, devoting himself to nursing his beloved wife back to health, only to discover that she had given her affections to another man. *I know he could do it,* he thought, *but there is more to this than a love affair and I cannot see it.*

~

"A Catholic funeral?" asked Gabriel. "Are you sure?"

"Mrs Webb insisted," said Cuthbert, holding out his beaker for water. "Be a good fellow, would you?" Gabriel took the cup from the man's clawed hands and went in search of the enamel jug Dominic always kept full. "She said he had told her once that he was born and brought up Catholic but had drifted away as a young man. Something about not believing a loving God could allow such misery in the world."

Gabriel rolled his eyes then wished he could be a little more understanding. There must have been thousands of men and women who could no longer believe in a loving God for just that reason. "I had not realised his body had been released."

"Oh yes—thank you, son." Cuthbert drank gratefully. More guilt. Gabriel had been late arriving at the infirmary for duty, and Cuthbert had been left alone longer than he ought. "Anyway, Father Abbot said that he would see to it."

"But who is paying for it?" Gabriel persisted. "The man was virtually penniless."

"I gather Mrs Webb is paying for the stone. She said she could not bear the thought of a young man who had died such a terrible death being buried without all the proper ceremony." He closed his eyes, holding out the beaker again, this time for Gabriel to place on his bedside table since he could not stretch far enough himself. "Now, isn't that kind? The Church is full of good women like her performing these little acts of kindness. It makes one believe the world is not entirely doomed after all."

"Good night," said Gabriel, pulling the bed sheet up over Cuthbert's chest. "Sweet dreams."

The following morning, as the community was celebrating Mass, the peace of the abbey was again disturbed by calls and shouts for help coming from the outer gate. Abbot Ambrose made an irate signal for Gabriel to slip out so as to cause as little disruption as possible, and he stepped out of choir and out of the chapel as fast as he decently could. He had barely tiptoed through the door when he was accosted by a distraught woman he barely recognised. Her head was uncovered, revealing dull grey hair, unpinned and wild; behind her lay a trail of muddy footprints from shoes soiled as she had hurried across the field.

"Mrs Webb?"

"Oh Father, something terrible has happened!" she cried, clasping his arm as though she thought she would fall. "I am sorry to burst in like this, but I didn't know where to go. The cottage—"

Gabriel felt his stomach lurching. "Is someone hurt?" he demanded. "Is someone dead?"

She shook her head, "No, no. Not that. The house has been—I do not know the English word!" She clutched the sides of her head. "It has been—I do not know. Paint everywhere, filth, things broken—"

"Ransacked?"

"Yes, it's terrible. And that poor boy not yet in his grave!"

"Show me," said Gabriel, leading her outside. "We'll go together."

The grass was soaking wet beneath Gabriel's feet, and he was reminded that the weather had broken in the night. He had lain awake, disturbed by the sound of the rain drumming against the lead roof and wondered what unnoticed clues were being washed away because he had failed to spot them before it was too late. He was not surprised Mrs Webb's feet were so filthy. Rushing as she had, she was fortunate not to have slipped. "You know, if no one was injured or dead you would have been better off going straight to the police," suggested Gabriel, pausing to allow her to keep up with him. "We will need to call them anyway."

"I do not like the police very much," said Mrs Webb. "Never have I liked men like that."

"Applegate's harmless enough. Well, perhaps not harmless, but definitely on the side of the angels."

"I do not trust him. I do not trust men like that. What if he thought I had done it and locked me up? God help me then."

Gabriel stopped again, watching as she closed the gap between them "When did you leave Germany, Mrs Weber?"

"After Kristallnacht. My husband was—" She spluttered to a stop and glowered at him. "I do not think that is fair, Father."

"It is Mrs Weber, is it not?"

They regarded one another through the shadowy morning light. "Why did you hide your name?" asked Gabriel, "When you settled in the village, you said you were Austrian. Why?"

"Because." Her eyes brimmed over again. "Because the English do not hate Austrians, but they do hate Germans. They will always hate them. Why shouldn't they?"

"I don't hate you."

Mrs Weber shook her head impatiently. "I could not tell a few good people the truth and a story to everyone else. You know it is not so easy."

"What happened to your husband?"

"It was his heart," she said, looking up at him as though to gauge whether or not she still had Gabriel's sympathy. "He tried to help a friend whose shop was being looted. There was fighting. He was not hurt. I thought he was all right. But then, next morning I awoke—I found him dead."

Gabriel touched Mrs Weber's arm. "I'm sorry. You think it was the shock?"

She smiled. "Oh no, I don't think it was that. He didn't want to live any more. A broken heart."

They were within sight of the cottage, and Gabriel could

already see the door swinging on its broken hinges. He took Mrs Weber by the arm and helped her to the entrance, but he could feel her edging back a little as they stepped inside. "Someone's made a good job of this," he said to nobody in particular.

It seemed to him that the cottage was becoming more and more of a waking nightmare. The carnage he remembered—the blood on the floor, the suffocatingly oppressive atmosphere—lingered like the last threads of smoke from a dying fire, but the vandal who had burst in had done his level best to destroy whatever had been left intact. The simple furnishings that had been overturned were broken and splintered from being kicked, stamped upon or hurled against the wall; the paintings on the walls had been slashed and torn, including the unframed picture of the red woman. Around the walls, every spare inch of plaster was covered in swastikas, clumsily daubed in red paint, as though the whole act of vandalism had been carried out in one short outburst of frenzied rage.

"All his paintings," Mrs Weber lamented, "every good thing he ever made—all destroyed."

Gabriel's attention was drawn to the painting of the red woman. The small, sharp blade of a penknife had punctured the canvas many times, but the woman's face had barely been touched. "Mrs Weber," said Gabriel, not looking away from the picture. "Are you going to tell me what happened to your son?"

Mrs Weber hurried to the doorway, only to stop abruptly a few inches from the outside. It had begun to rain again, so heavily that it was impossible to see further than a few yards into the distance. If she went outside she would be drenched within seconds. "How long have you known, Father?" she asked, stepping back to the shelter of the destroyed room.

"You are a good woman, Mrs Weber, but it was going a little beyond the realms of kindness to insist upon a Catholic funeral for a man you did not know from Adam, let alone promising to pay for his tombstone. Why should you be so keen for him to be remembered?"

She began to sink to her knees; Gabriel rushed forwards to stop her from falling, fearing that she would get blood on her clothing. She buried her head in his shoulder, stifling a hideous, animal wail that seemed to go on for an eternity. "He was not a Nazi, Father!" she gasped. "He was a hero, he was sent to prison."

Gabriel looked round for some way to make her more comfortable. The rainstorm would not pass in a hurry, and they had a great deal to talk about. In the absence of unsoiled blankets or furniture, he tore down a curtain and placed it in the far corner of the room, as far from the open door as he could. While she sat down, he went over and attempted to close the door to keep out the rain and wind. The lock of the door had been kicked in so violently that in the end the only way he could force the door to remain closed was to jam it shut with a piece of broken furniture.

"Why did he not leave Germany with you?"

"I wanted him to come," she said distractedly. "I begged him and begged him to come with me. He said it was his duty to stay. He said it was right I go somewhere safe, but he would find some way to fight Hitler. He was a patriotic boy, but in a good way. I told you, he was a hero."

"I'm sure he was. When did you last hear from him?"

"February 1941, I still have the letter. Later he was arrested by the Gestapo. They sent him to a camp. His next letter came after the War."

"What did he tell you?"

"That he was well and free. He wanted to come to England." Her face darkened almost imperceptibly. "He said he had had some trouble and would be better if he change his name, better if people not know him as my son."

"Did he ever tell you what the trouble was?"

Mrs Weber shook her head morosely. "No. He would not talk. They had done something terrible to him, and he was frightened. He—" She began twisting the corner of the curtain that was covering her. "He trusted no one, not even me. I said, the War is over, there is nothing to fear, but he would not listen. You have no idea, Father, how it feels to be pushed away by your own son when you know he needs you."

Gabriel started. The image of Dr Paige and his frail, silent wife flashed through his mind. "The War has come between so many," he mused, "Dr Paige—"

"No," she said firmly enough to stop him. "Do not say that murderer's name to me."

Gabriel felt the increasingly familiar sensation of his stomach knotting up. "You think he killed your son?"

"Of course," she answered brutally, shaking off the curtain as though she had suddenly tired of being coddled. "There's more. My son knew that woman before he came here."

"Oh?" Gabriel tried to sound as nonchalant as possible. This was not at all what he had wanted to hear, and he suspected it was going to get a good deal worse. "What makes you say that?"

Mrs Weber looked at him with something like pity. "Father, you know Dr Paige killed my son and tried to kill his wife. You do not want to believe it because you like him."

"That's unfair, I merely—"

"No!" she exclaimed, giving him a triumphant smile that made him shiver. You liked *them* because they were the way you think people should be. The frail little wife; the strong, loyal husband. But she belonged to Johannes years before she ever belonged to that man. I am sure of it. He didn't come to this village to be near his old mother. He had been searching for her."

"Madam, I would think very carefully before accusing Marie Paige of adultery."

"Oh no, no!" protested Mrs Weber quickly, the smile vanishing. "She was not a a bad woman, I am sure. You misunderstand."

"You said—"

"I *mean*, I think she came to see Johannes to tell him to go away, but Dr Paige did not know that. He thought the worst."

"I find it very hard to believe a man like that could have done it."

"The man is a brute," she said, as though the point were blatantly obvious, "I saw bruises on her arm, big bruises. Maybe she had more because he stopped me taking off her jacket, didn't he? He is a big man. What a man like him can do when he is angry!"

Gabriel got up and reached out a hand to help Mrs Weber to her feet. "The rain has stopped. I think I had better report this incident to the police before I return to the abbey."

Mrs Weber waved away his offer of help and stood up. "No, I will tell the police. I rather go to them than they come to me."

"I will accompany you if you prefer," offered Gabriel, walking out beside her. The air still felt heavy with moisture, and it was so dark it could easily have been dusk already.

"It's quite all right. Go back to your cloister."

Gabriel watched Mrs Weber slipping and sliding her way in the direction of the village. He was honestly not sure whether she had been speaking in the matter-of-fact way of a person using their second language or whether she had intended to insult him.

~

"I hate to say this, Gabriel," said Dominic, as they stood at the infirmary sink, washing their hands, "but my heart sank when Father Abbot said you would be assisting me today. You really ought to drop the whole thing, you know."

"And leave an innocent man to hang?"

Dominic threw Gabriel a towel. "You'd serve that poor man far better if you encouraged him to confess."

"It's a simple enough question, Dominic. Could anything else have caused her injuries?"

Dominic rolled his eyes. He was not an impatient man by nature but Gabriel had talked of nothing else since the murder had first been discovered and he had answered a number of "simple questions" already. "To have sustained injuries as severe as that, the house would have had to have fallen on her," he declared. "I do not recall that Mrs Paige was dragged out from beneath three feet of rubble."

"I don't mean that, you numpty! I meant the bruising on her arm. Dr Paige said it was caused by iron injections. Is that likely?" he asked. Dominic was silent. "Is it plausible?"

"Yes," he admitted, "it is plausible. Any needle can cause bruising, and some people are more susceptible than others. It just feels a little too convenient an explanation under the circumstances. We have only his word for it that he gave her iron injections in the first place."

"Did she look anaemic to you?"

Dominic put down the iodine bottle he had been in the process of opening. "She was so anaemic I am amazed she was capable of walking. Think how deathly pale and tired she was, always short of breath. Classic anaemia symptoms."

"Well then!" said Gabriel, as though Dominic had conceded a point. "The evidence speaks for itself!"

"Gabriel," he said gently, "you haven't asked me the other obvious question, but I'll answer it anyway. She had all the symptoms of being a battered wife too. Fragile, nervy, stick thin, a husband forever hovering at her side whenever she was likely to speak with anyone else. When did you ever see her alone?"

Gabriel sighed. "When her husband was at work."

"Quite." Dominic watched his friend's shoulders droop as the energy drained out of him. "Look, if it helps, Dr Paige does not strike me as a wife-beater either. I can't quite imagine him actually hitting her—I just can't see it somehow—but there have been rumours swirling about the village for months."

"I sincerely hope you have not been listening to idle gossip?" Gabriel choked a little on his own hypocrisy. "You know what Merriott's like."

"The words pot, kettle and black spring to mind! You know part of you believed him too."

"Well . . ." A charge of hypocrisy was second only to being called a liar in Gabriel's book—even when he knew it was true—and he struggled to defend himself. "One had to consider why a woman like that walked about as though she had the devil at her heels, that's all. I never really believed it." He heard Dominic give a quiet groan of exasperation. "Look, I'm the one who has been trying to find another hypothesis from the start!"

Dominic looked sadly at his friend. "All I mean is that, in the end, you know as well as I do how little we really know about what's going on in a marriage. People learn to put a face on things."

"It all feels so *wrong*!" wailed Gabriel. "Can't you feel it too? Every bone in my body tells me he's innocent but the facts keep screaming at me."

"Gabriel, do your duty as a priest. Go to him and beg him to confess. If he pleads guilty at his trial . . ."

"There's nothing meek and mild about the man, I can imagine him being violent if he absolutely had to be. But the only time I can honestly see him hurting anyone would be if he were protecting Marie."

"Gabriel—"

"I can fully imagine him beating a man to within an inch of his life simply for *threatening* Marie, but this feels wrong."

Dominic swallowed hard. "Marie was the one who was beaten and no, there is no possibility whatsoever that she was the victim of an unfortunate accident. She was attacked by someone who had no intention other than to do her serious harm. Quite probably to kill her. That's a fact." Dominic paused, expecting words of protest, but Gabriel merely hung his head. "Spare your pity for the victims, Gabriel, not the man who attacked them. I've told you already, it was a horrible crime. He deliberately killed a man as slowly as possible then turned on a woman who must have struggled and pleaded for her life." Gabriel looked up at him in surprise. "What?"

"The paper boy never said that he heard a struggle," said Gabriel. "He mentioned a shot; that was all."

"The . . . the shot would have carried further," said Dominic, but he was flummoxed as usual and knew Gabriel had noticed. "The sound of the shot, I mean. There must have been a violent struggle, you said the room was a mess. Gabriel, she would have been in agony, he fractured limbs, she would have been screaming . . . "

"There were no screams. All that was heard was a shot."

"You're clutching at straws again. The child was scared; he may have forgotten the details."

"If straws are all there are, I shall have to keep clutching at them, shan't I?" Gabriel suddenly became aware of how loudly they were talking and dropped his voice. "But it's an awfully long time since I have had any certainties about this at all, even that this is really a murder we are investigating."

"You are not investigating anything," came a terse, clipped voice the two men knew all too well. They turned to the doorway where Abbot Ambrose was standing watching them. Neither could have guessed how long he had been listening, but the last ten seconds would have been hard enough to explain. "Dominic, get about your business. You have been delayed quite long enough. Gabriel, come with me." Abbot Ambrose gestured with his head for Gabriel to follow him out of the room. As soon as they were safely in the corridor, Ambrose turned to confront him. "I have received a complaint from Mrs Webb that you caused her unnecessary distress this morning when you should have been assisting her."

"Her name is Mrs Weber. She's—"

"That is no business of yours," Abbot Ambrose retorted. "You had no business asking her personal questions. As soon as she had shown you what she had found, you should have accompanied her directly to the police station."

"Father Abbot, it was pouring with rain, she would have caught her death."

"Instead, you interrogated her about her past and you did not accompany her to the police."

"She didn't want me to go with her."

"That is hardly surprising after the way you behaved, is it? She never made it as far as the police station. Someone found her wandering about in hysterics and took her to the police themselves thinking she had been the victim of a crime. It was Inspector Applegate who encouraged her to telephone me."

Gabriel took in this latest catastrophe and could think of no other response than to throw up his hands. "Forgive me, Father Abbot, I have made a mess of this. I will go to the inspector and explain everything myself."

Abbot Ambrose narrowed his eyes and Gabriel knew the case was useless. "You will do no such thing. I forbid you to leave the abbey." With that, Abbot Ambrose turned on his heel and marched out of sight with the determination of a man who really should not be followed.

"Bad luck," said Dominic, poking his head out of the infirmary door. "What are you going to do now?"

Gabriel inclined his head. "How would you feel about a spot of breaking and entering?"

Dominic shook his head in exasperation. "Please don't do anything foolish. You'll get yourself arrested at the rate you're going."

"Well, how about it?"

"I'm not sure a cripple like me is quite the man you want. How about a wiry little soul like Gerard?"

11

"The abbot'll have your guts for garters," muttered Gerard, as they scarpered out of the abbey. "I mean it. You're supposed to be under obedience."

"We'll be back in under an hour. No one will notice."

"What's that got to do with it?" protested Gerard. "He said stay in the abbey. How you going to explain this?"

Gabriel could feel his heart thumping against his ribs. The chief difficulty with slipping out of the abbey was the amount of open ground they had to cover before being safely out of sight. Even moving quickly, their black figures were so conspicuous, and there were so many windows a monk might be glancing through at any one time; avoiding detection was tricky to say the very least. The only consolation he had was that, from the back, one monk looked very much like another—except for Dominic, whose limp gave him away the moment he took a step. All said and done, it had been a good suggestion of his to ask Gerard to accompany him on his latest mad escapade.

"Look, Gerard, I'm beginning to think you must have been one of those insufferable little prigs at school who always brought the teacher an apple."

Gerard jabbed his friend in the ribs. "Since you ask, I was

expelled for smoking ciggies behind the bike shed during algebra. What's that to do with the price of fish?"

"Stop behaving like the voice of conscience then. The abbot will understand."

"It's pride," Gerard persisted. "Educated men like you always think the rules don't apply to them. You weren't expelled from school yourself, were you?"

"Certainly not, I was a prefect. For about five minutes."

Gerard chuckled. "Rumbled you, did they?"

"No," sighed Gabriel, opening the gate that led to the main road. Gerard ignored him and vaulted the low stone wall. "I didn't have the guts to cane the little ones. I've never liked violence."

"Aaaaaw!" came the infuriating answer. "You big softie! I knew it would be something like that."

Gabriel felt himself blushing. "Look, it's mad asking boys to punish other boys. I have never liked the idea. I used to have to ask one of the other prefects to do it and that felt cowardly." Gabriel could hear the barely suppressed snigger in Gerard's voice and suspected he would never hear the last of it. "I don't know what you find so funny."

Gerard gave a conciliatory smile. "Nothing to be ashamed of, Gabbers. You're a gentle soul, that's all. Anyway, what you looking for?"

They were walking in the direction of the Paiges' home; Gabriel heard the faint chiming of the abbey clock. "We have very little time." He glanced at Gerard and was disconcerted to see him staring downwards, apparently lost in thought. "What's the matter?"

"Alastair Brennan's the matter. Keep walking, I feel as though we're being watched."

"If Father Abbot's behind us, I'll deny any knowledge of your existence."

"Just shurrup and listen! When you were a prefect you got someone else to do your dirty work for you."

Gabriel winced. "Steady on, that's a bit strong! I stopped being a prefect . . ."

"Never mind the rights and wrongs of it now, but that's what you did, didn't you?"

"Yes," answered Gabriel forlornly, "there was always some thug in my form who was happy enough to bash the little blighters if I couldn't. Gerry, you're not suggesting—"

"He could have done it. He was near the scene of the crime."

"It's even harder for me to imagine Alastair Brennan hurting Marie than the good doctor."

"But he was there and he's never explained his presence there to your satisfaction, has he? You said so yourself."

They had walked around the back of a row of cottages and began trudging in single file along the narrow footpath between an extensive hedge of brambles heaving with blackberries and the low fences separating the path from the modest back gardens of the cottages. Most were well kept, and virtually all contained vegetable patches of varying degrees of abundance. Some of the gardens had a shed. "Gabriel," pestered Gerard, "if your instincts are correct and Dr Paige was not capable of hurting his own wife even if he wanted to, he could have asked someone else."

"Not now, Gerry."

"He's a clever enough man to do that."

Gabriel raised a finger to his lips. "Be quiet. I've lost my bearings. Never come to the house this way before."

"This is crackers, we'll be seen!"

"Will you shut your mouth?" But Gabriel was perturbed by the sight of two small boys playing in the garden he believed was next door to the Paiges'. They were aged around six and eight, he judged, occupied in a shambolic attempt at turning two old chairs and a blanket into a tent, but not so absorbed that they would have failed to notice the sound of footsteps. Two round faces glanced at the men. "Hello there, boys!" said Gabriel as naturally as he could. "Is that the doctor's house over there?"

"Yeah," said the older of the two, holding out his hands like a monster from a ham horror film. "The killer's house!"

"Well—"

"Mother says, who would have thought we were living next to another Dr Crippin?" continued the boy, imitating the slightly shrill, gossipy tone of a nosy housewife, complete with rolling eyes and pursed lips. "Makes the blood run cold, doesn't it? And he seemed so nice."

Gabriel could sense Gerard struggling not to laugh—partly because of nerves—and he turned to face the back of the house. The back room of the ground floor was the kitchen; Gabriel could just make out the black chimney of the stove through the window. His eyes darted up to the window of the second storey, and he saw the unmistakeable flicker of a shadow as someone moved across the upstairs landing. "Is there someone at home?" he asked nonchalantly.

"Only Mr Merriott," answered the boy, "doing some building work while it's empty. Let himself in this morning."

"Really? Well, we'll talk to Mr Merriott then." He opened the garden gate, stood aside to let a reluctant Gerard in and made for the back door. "Just walk in as though you own the place," Gabriel hissed under his breath. "It never fails."

"This is madness, it's broad daylight," answered Gerard, when they had stepped quietly into the kitchen and Gabriel had closed the door behind them. "How are we going to explain this when the police arrive?"

"I don't think it counts as breaking and entering if someone else has done the breaking." They froze at the sound of heavy footsteps creaking down the stairs, each man holding his breath. On an invisible signal, Gabriel advanced towards the foot of the stairs and looked calmly in Merriott's direction. "Mr Merriott," he said, calmly, "we both have some explaining to do."

It took several uneasy seconds for Gordon Merriott to recover himself enough to answer. "I was only looking."

"Indeed. Why don't you make yourself at home? You seem to have gone some way to doing so already."

"I was only looking," Merriott repeated, sitting down on the stairs with the two monks flanking him like acolytes. "The door wasn't even locked."

"You were no more here on honest business than we were," answered Gabriel politely. "Why should Dr Paige ask you to do work on his house when he may be hanged before the year is out?"

"What was you here for then, Father?" leered Merriott, glaring at him from beneath a shapeless black hat that formed some kind of makeshift disguise. "Inspector Applegate send you, did he?"

"Why don't you take that ridiculous hat off, Merriott? It didn't fool those children out there, and I prefer to see all of a man's face if possible."

Merriott snatched the hat off his head and continued to glare at Gabriel with the rage of a man who fears a lost profit far more than arrest. He knew Gabriel was in no position to report him. "If you must know, I was looking for clues meself—no different from what you're playing at."

You're a liar, thought Gabriel. He said, "Really? What were you hoping to find? The police will already have taken away anything useful, I suspect."

"If that's what y'thought, why d'you come here yourself then?" demanded Merriott, reasonably enough, as he got up and headed up the stairs.

"I thought they might have missed something, I suppose."

"Yes indeedy, Father, and you'd be right," he said, turning back to look at them over the landing bannister. "Take a look at this."

Merriott led them into the master bedroom, striding in with Gabriel and Gerard standing awkwardly in the doorway. For two trespassers, they both felt the same discomfort about entering a marital bedroom, all the more so when they saw the state it was in. The room was a mess, not destructively so in the way Pederson's cottage had been ransacked, but all the same it did not reflect the character of the rest of the house or its original occupants. Bedside drawers had been left open, the contents in a state of disarray after being hastily rifled through; the wardrobe doors were ajar with various articles of clothing tumbling through the gap. Around the edge of the bed, several boxes used for storage had been pulled out from under the bed, searched and left without the lids being properly replaced. An ottoman box in the corner had been similarly tampered with and left open.

"What's this all about?" asked Gerard, stepping gingerly inside to get a better look. "Was this the police?"

"No," said Gabriel, "they would have put things back or taken them away. Either this happened beforehand and the police thought it important enough not to interfere, or thieves have been here since Dr Paige was arrested."

"This is no thieving work," said Merriott. "Whoever ran round this room knew what they was looking for. Something precious they always kept hidden away just in case they was ever to need it."

Gabriel knew he was right. There was something about the organised chaos that pointed to Dr Paige's work. Nothing was broken or overturned. Drawers and cupboards and boxes were open, but the messiness suggested a person desperately searching for something and running off in the knowledge that he could return later to put the room to rights. The search itself had been fairly strategic. "We've got to get out of here," whispered Gerard, gulping with sudden panic. "We shouldn't be here. None of us were here, none of us saw one another."

"Merriott, may we talk further outside?" asked Gabriel. "He's right, we shouldn't linger here, it will be very serious for all of us if we're caught trespassing."

"Aye, come with me."

They rushed down the stairs, following Merriott's vast figure as he strode back through the kitchen into the garden. Gabriel was relieved to note that the boys had been called inside and were not there to witness their flight. Merriott waited until they were back on the footpath before stating quietly, "He was searching for his gun. It stands to reason."

"I'm not sure it does. Ow!" In his hurry to catch up with Merriott, Gabriel had lost his balance and caught his hand on a bramble as he reached out to steady himself. The thorny branch bit into the palm of his hand, which immediately started bleeding profusely. "Wait a minute!"

"Don't worry, hand wounds always look worse than they are," Gerard chimed in, handing Gabriel a handkerchief. "Here you go. Dominic told me."

"Thank you, Brother, that helps a lot. Just a minute, Merriott, why did it have to be a gun he was searching for?"

Merriott replaced his hat with a palpable sense of victory. "Think about it, Father. What else would a man hide away very carefully, but then forget where he'd stored it because he never needed it?"

"You're very sure he's the killer, aren't you?" Gabriel asked feebly, but the shock of cutting himself had made him feel pathetically light-headed. "May we stop a moment?"

Merriott ignored him and continued his march to the road. "Everyone knows he did it except you, Father. I know he did it."

"Saw him, did you?"

"Heard him." Merriott turned around to face them, so abruptly they almost collided head-on. "I know you think I'm a liar, Father, but it was true what I said I heard all them months back."

"I'm not sure I can . . ." His head swam. Gabriel blinked, sucked in a deep breath. "I'm not sure . . . I can remember . . ." He saw millions of grains of rice before his eyes, then darkness, then light, then darkness again. Finally, the world snapped back into focus.

"That night when I was walking home, I passed their house. You should've heard her screams."

Gerard noticed Gabriel's confusion and stepped in himself. "She could have had nightmares. Perhaps she was in pain, you can't be sure of anything."

"She was *screaming*. D'you hear? I'm an old soldier and I know when someone's in danger. I know when someone's having a bad dream and when they're scared to death. She was scared. *Pleading* with him to leave her alone. 'Don't! Please don't! Don't do it, don't do it!' I wish I'd put a shoulder to the front door and rescued her meself."

"Dr Paige said his wife was afraid of—"

"How much more evidence d'you need before you take the blinkers off?" thundered Merriott, jabbing Gabriel in the chest. "Everyone's laughing at you running round in circles trying to prove a guilty man innocent. Your boss ought to lock you up!"

I should think he's had the same thought himself, thought Gabriel, watching dazedly as Merriott stormed out of sight. "Gerry, go home."

"You should come too," said Gerard gently. "You don't look well and heaven knows what Father Abbot'll have to say about this. I shouldn't have encouraged you."

"I needed no encouragement." He closed his eyes and counted to five, feeling misery sticking to him like mud and trying to shrug it off. "You must go back. I don't want you getting into trouble because I couldn't see the wood for the trees. You don't have to cover for me either if I'm missed, I'll explain myself later."

Gerard began to walk reluctantly away, only to turn again as a thought returned to him. "Gabriel?"

"Yes."

"What I said about Alastair Brennan. Forget about it. If Dr Paige left the house with a gun, he obviously didn't ask anyone else to get involved. I don't want to drag another man's name into all this."

Gabriel stood alone, hot and light-headed, contemplating his next move. He had almost forgotten that fear felt so much like sickness. *I shall not fear the terrors of the night . . . or the noonday devil . . . or the arrow, the arrow.* He felt overcome by the one horror he had always feared: he was making a mess of everything again, and someone was going to get hurt. Gabriel glanced down at his hand and noticed that the blood had seeped through Gerard's flimsy handkerchief. He would have to ask Dominic to take a look at it in case he finished up with a bout of tetanus just to make his day complete. *What am I not seeing, oh God?* he cried inwardly. *What am I not seeing?*

12

Alastair Brennan acted surprised when he answered the door and found a wounded Father Gabriel standing woefully on the doorstep, but he had seen him coming as he sat at the sitting room window. He had drained and hidden his glass, and slipped a peppermint into his mouth to disguise the smell before moving towards the door.

"Good day, Father," he said with forced cheerfulness. "What can I do for you?" He looked at the blood-stained handkerchief covering Gabriel's hand. "You have been in the wars."

"I don't suppose I could requisition your kitchen sink for a moment, could I?" asked Gabriel, stepping inside. "I've cut my hand on some brambles."

"Of course. Come in."

Alastair led Gabriel to the kitchen and began a half-hearted search for some means to dress the wound whilst Gabriel ran his hand under the cold tap. "Much obliged."

"Not at all, that looks quite nasty. Here." He brought out a bottle of iodine, which he set down on the work surface, then rummaged in a drawer for his roll of discoloured bandages. "Can't say I make much use of this first aid kit, fortunately, but old habits die hard. One never knows when one might need it."

"Indeed." Gabriel could not control the urge to flinch as Alastair splashed iodine over his hand. "I think I might burst into tears."

"It does make the eyes water," admitted Alastair, attempting to unroll a bandage around Gabriel's hand whilst Gabriel held the end. "You'll need a tetanus shot by the look of things."

Gabriel grimaced. "I sincerely hope not, I'm not overly fond of needles."

Alastair chuckled. "Nobody is. But I wouldn't mind if you really were sincere for a moment." Gabriel gave him a bemused look. Alastair had the disconcerting English habit of making an accusatory, even outright offensive remark with an unwaveringly affable tone that virtually disguised it. "Oh come along, Father, do you really expect me to believe that you knocked on my door because you cut your hand? You might just as easily have found your way back to the abbey. Now, what was it you wanted?"

Gabriel sighed. "I'm not much good at all this. Very well, might we sit down?"

Alastair directed him to the sitting room. "Why not? Find anything interesting at Maison Paige? Please don't look surprised again. I know there is a blackberry bush at the back of their garden. Marie made a disastrous batch of blackberry jam last autumn. Clever girl, but her talents lie elsewhere."

"Was that another of Dr Paige's ideas?" ventured Gabriel.

"I dare say."

Gabriel held up his bandaged hand. "Marie has a scar

on her hand in almost the same place. Do you know where she got it?"

It was Alastair's turn to look puzzled. "No. I know the one you mean, it's quite noticeable. I'm sure she said she couldn't remember. One always had to be a little careful with Marie. The past was a bit of a minefield."

"Is. She's not dead as far as I am aware. Did she have it when she was at school?"

"How the devil should I—" He stopped in his tracks. "Wait. It's on her right hand, isn't it?"

"Yes."

"I'm not sure I can—"

"It's all right. Take your time."

Alastair's mind went back to those dusty memories before scandal and the War shattered everything. He was seated in a row with the other teachers—mostly nuns—on the stage at the front of the hall for Friday assembly. In front of him, sitting in alphabetical order, form by form starting with the youngest, were rows and rows of girls in the brown and green uniform of Saint Genevieve School. Girls who had misbehaved during the previous week were being called up by the headmistress in groups of three or four. He saw Marie aged about twelve; her round, normally impish face bearing a look of cool defiance as she climbed up the four steps to the platform. He got a very clear sight of her because the headmistress was standing almost directly in front of him. He saw her stretch out her hands, palms upwards, before he hastily looked away.

"It's one of those moments I will never forget," he added after describing the incident.

"Brennan, you're very white. What is it?"

"That's how he did it," he said to no one in particular, before turning to Gabriel. "That's how he made her bleed." It was the first time Alastair had given Gabriel a clear view of his face, and Gabriel was shocked at how haggard he looked. "Father, for pity's sake, you couldn't fool a child. You *knew* it was me."

"I guessed it was you who smashed up Pederson's cottage. You sabotaged his painting of Marie but didn't touch the face. You couldn't bear to, could you?"

"How did you know it was her? It was so abstract and her face is in profile, with that scarf covering her head."

"I only recognised it as an old portrait of her because of what you did to it."

"You saw that it was painted in blood, I suppose?"

Gabriel clenched his uninjured hand to stop himself reacting. "No, I thought it was made to look like blood. I'm not much of an artist, I'm afraid."

"I only realised how he'd done it just then when you drew attention to Marie's scar. He must have made her squeeze a piece of glass or something. I didn't make the connection before, it is all so twisted." Alastair massaged his temples as though trying to stay awake. "You know I've had a skinful today, but I'm not nearly as drunk as I need to be."

"Brennan, you know how much trouble you are in. I suggest you try to keep your head clear."

"*I'm* in trouble?" he echoed, staring at Gabriel in disbelief. "I have not hurt anyone. I merely drew the attention of every stupid member of this village to the sort of man Pederson was! I knew he was a Nazi the moment I heard Merriott say those disgraceful things about Marie."

"Brennan, he was a prisoner of the Nazis. He had the tattoo on his arm to prove it. Whatever else he was."

"Do you know so little about how it happened? He may have been a prisoner to begin with, but by the time Marie fell afoul of him, he had been turned into a guard. Somehow or other, he finished up on the wrong side. I need another drink."

"No." Gabriel got up to stand between Alastair and the drinks cabinet. "If you need to calm your nerves, light yourself a cigarette. You may need to come with me to the police station later, and it will be better for your sake if you are sober when Applegate questions you."

Alastair stared unblinkingly ahead, but tears began to course down his cheeks in spite of his best efforts. "I'm sorry, you must think me a raving lunatic. I haven't been sleeping. You see, Marie said something months ago. It was . . . well, it was one of those rare moments when she suddenly started talking and we both stopped to listen to her. She was like that. She was so silent about it all, and then sometimes—sometimes out of the blue—something would be said that would start her talking; and it would all come out like a dam bursting."

"She mentioned him?"

"No, not personally, she never mentioned names. She . . . she just said that she thought . . . she thought perhaps one day she could forgive the SS everything. It was so very hard but . . . but perhaps she could. But God have mercy on her, she said, she wasn't sure she could forgive the Kapos. She couldn't understand how a prisoner could be prevailed upon to hurt another prisoner. It was like attacking one's own family, she said."

Gabriel buried his head in his hands. "I couldn't see beyond that serial number."

"She said the Kapos were worse than the SS. She started talking about the most horrible things. Poor Dickie was in a terrible state afterwards. When that louse Merriott started talking in the shop, I knew what he had really heard. That, well, that reference to crowds and coming for her. I knew he must have singled her out back then."

"When did you decide to kill him?"

Alastair closed his eyes. It was almost childish, as though he found it easier to tell the truth if he could pretend Gabriel was not in the room. "You knew I was lying about being near the scene of the murder. I do wander in the early morning sometimes, but that morning I knew exactly where I was going. I packed a carving knife and made for Pederson's cottage."

"You should have gone directly to the police, Brennan."

Alastair opened his eyes momentarily simply to give Gabriel the benefit of a contemptuous glance. "They wouldn't have done anything, not in time anyway. I just wanted to protect Marie. I knew he had come to claim her. I've never been able to protect her as I wanted. I couldn't stop her being expelled. I couldn't stop her getting hurt, being—well, I don't suppose any of us will know exactly what they did to her, though I can guess. But I knew this time I could stop him."

"What did you imagine he meant to do?"

"How should I know? Silence her? Destroy her life all over again? How should I know? I just knew he meant to hurt her, and this time I was damn well going to stop him. Is that so wrong?"

"Did you kill him?"

Alastair broke down again, which answered the question eloquently enough. "He was already dead. I thought, 'Oh God I'm too late.' I thought they were both dead. There was so much blood. I thought I'd failed her again. After that, I panicked. I just ran."

Gabriel sprang to his feet. "Don't lie to me all over again." Alastair recoiled. "I'm not the only one who couldn't fool a child," Gabriel snapped. "You must know if you refuse to tell me the truth you will answer to Applegate, and he will be most unimpressed by your stories."

"Father, I am telling the truth!"

"If that was all you did, you could surely have told the police as much," Gabriel said. He could blame his sudden rush of anger on all sorts of things—his hatred of deceit, his desperation to put right his own mistakes, even his own intense fear—but he could barely stop himself from shouting. "A woman you claim to love, whom you claim to have wanted to protect, lies dead—or so you think—alongside a man you had intended to kill yourself, and you simply *run?* Even if you did not have the guts to tell the police what had happened right at the start, you have had plenty of time to tell them the truth. Did it not occur to you that you might have been implicated?"

Alastair was huddled up in his chair like a little boy. He was not weeping, but he made no attempt at answering. For a while Gabriel could not work out whether Alastair was stalling for time or was genuinely too distressed to answer. He looked up slowly, but he was still trembling and made no effort to conceal it. "Do not shout at me again," he said quietly. "You've no idea what I have been through."

"Brennan, I know this is very hard for you to talk about, but—"

"Alastair. Please."

"Thank you. *Alastair*, the police will no doubt notice this, so I think I should draw your attention to it. I knew you had attacked that painting because you could not bring yourself to stick a knife into Marie's face. It was a peculiar detail, but one that led me to your door. The person who attacked Marie in the flesh hardly touched her face either. It might be an unfortunate coincidence, but—"

Alastair rose to his feet. "I'm a cripple, for crying out loud! I couldn't inflict that much damage on another human being even if I wanted to!"

"Marie is small even for a woman and very weak," stated Gabriel, "as well you know. A single blow would have been enough to get her on the ground, and not even a very forceful one, after which she would have been completely helpless."

"Do you truly think I could have done that to her—after all I've told you?"

"I am simply drawing your attention to another peculiar detail in this story that might lead Applegate to your door next time. For a man to be capable of doing something quite so brutal and yet not to be able to bring himself to damage her face does rather suggest the attacker had some sort of feelings for her, albeit disordered."

Alastair stepped as close to Gabriel as he dared. When he spoke, he was as clear and as quiet as he could manage. "I have told you, I thought they were already dead. I never touched either of them. I blundered in on that terrible scene and then I ran."

Gabriel adopted the same manner as his opponent. "You can do considerably better than that, Alastair. Yours is not the panic of an innocent man. I can only help you if you tell me what really happened."

Alastair did not break eye contact. He stood stock still, breathing as though he had just run a steeplechase, fighting an inner battle Gabriel wanted desperately for him to win. "All right," he said decisively, "what if I were to tell you that I did kill Pederson, Father? When I approached the cottage, I could hear Marie screaming. It was my worst nightmare. I ran as fast as I could, but by the time I was able to force open the door, she was quiet. I saw Pederson kicking her. I thought—I believed she was already dead, but he kept kicking her and stamping on her. There was no other way to stop him."

Gabriel placed a hand on Alastair's shoulder. "That was very brave," he said, gently, "you are a most loyal friend. But as far as I know, nobody has ever shot a man dead with a carving knife."

Alastair crumpled again, so quickly Gabriel had to assist him back into his chair. "For pity's sake leave me alone!" he wailed, burying his head. "Just go!"

"For the last time, Alastair, what *actually happened*?" Silence; Alastair refused to raise his head. "Or perhaps I should tell you what happened? Would you prefer that?" Gabriel paused for an answer, but Alastair did not move. "Very well, you did indeed go to the cottage that morning with the intention of killing Pederson, but as you said, you arrived too late. You looked at those two bodies; one a man you hated more than any other person on this earth—and let's face it, Alastair, you are a good hater—the other a woman for whom you would lay down your life. It does not occur to you in your distress that you might be implicated in the deaths if you are spotted at the scene. You are too preoccupied to consider your own safety. Because you know the killer. You see a British service revolver and you recognise it as belonging to your friend Dr Richard Paige. You know he keeps a gun in the house, he has no doubt confided as much to you in the past. You know he has been here. Worst of all, you realise that he has misunderstood his wife's dealings with Pederson and has been driven to commit an act that would ordinarily have been impossible for such a man to contemplate."

"Father . . ."

"You decide to hide the evidence, but that is not so easy for a man in your condition to do. You cannot risk carrying it away with you. Even if it were possible to do so, you might be apprehended with not one, but two weapons on your person. So you endeavour to throw it out the window and perhaps retrieve it at a later date. That way, you can protect your friend and avoid anyone knowing that you were ever there."

Alastair shook his head wearily. "It was no easy matter to get that wretched window open one-handed." Gabriel noticed his eyes glistening again, but he did not break down. "I want you to do something for me, Father."

"I will if I can," he replied.

"I want you to walk away from this and stay away. I am going to confess. I am going to tell Applegate exactly what I have told you."

"Alastair . . ."

"You are the only one who knows about the carving

knife. I will say I stole the gun. I will not hang for shooting a man dead in defence of another, and I'm not sure it matters anyway. I think you understand why I am doing this."

"Greater love hath no man?"

"Yes."

"No, Alastair," said Gabriel firmly, turning to leave. "Don't be a blithering idiot."

Alastair rushed in front of him blocking his way. "I have to do this!"

"Learn the difference between martyrdom and rank stupidity. Making a false confession benefits no one."

"He could not have hurt Marie. If he killed Pederson it was for a good reason."

Gabriel stood with his back to the closed front door. "If Dr Paige killed Pederson to protect his wife, why has he not said so? The man is facing the gallows. He has every reason to own up but he is refusing to speak."

"Then there was some other reason! Or if he did attack them both, he was acting completely out of character, in a moment of madness!"

Gabriel looked at Alastair Brennan's sunken face and felt a miserable sense of the hopelessness of the situation. No one could possibly come out of this well. "Whatever his motives, if Dr Paige is the guilty man, then Dr Paige must do his own penance." Gabriel opened the door and stepped out into a street swathed in cold sunlight. He still felt afraid. "And I must do mine," he whispered before going on his way.

13

I may as well hang for sheep as for lamb, thought Gabriel woe-fully, as he walked in the direction of the police station. It must have been his monastic training, but every time the abbey bell chimed in the distance, he heard its rebuke as though it were as loud as a shrieking air raid siren. He knew he must have been missed by now, probably for well over an hour, and there could be no hope of sneaking back inside. What depressed him most was the thought of having been the author of his own misfortune. It would be quite under-standable if he were sent away from the abbey after all this —heaven knows, it might even do him some good—but the prospect of exile horrified him almost as much as the hangman might. It would be a death of sorts if it came, very much like being forcibly torn away from one's own family. Gabriel knew he could not let his mind settle on the idea for the moment or it would paralyse him when he still had work to do. There was one final task for him to perform before he went back to the abbey to account for his actions and that was to prepare Dr Paige to do the same.

~

"No," said Applegate, as soon as Gabriel walked into his office.

"You haven't asked me what I want yet," Gabriel pointed out in a hurt voice.

"We have a date for the doctor's trial. Nothing more to be said."

"I'm here as a priest," said Gabriel, prompting an incredulous snort from Applegate. "No. I *am* here as a priest this time. Mostly. May I ask, is Dr Paige entering a guilty plea?"

"No of course he isn't," Applegate retorted. "He's been pleading innocence ever since we nicked him."

"Is there still time for him to change it?"

Applegate looked up in surprise. "Plenty, but he don't want to speak to you."

"He might if I ask nicely?"

"I don't want to speak to you," barked Dr Paige severely, when Gabriel appeared in his cell after much clatter of keys and creaking of doors. "I think I made that quite clear the last time you tried to trick me into confessing."

"You have a beard worthy of Abraham," said Gabriel in a feeble attempt at a joke. In all honesty, Dr Paige looked more like the Grim Reaper than a biblical patriarch.

"They won't let me have a razor blade in case I try to top myself," Dr Paige explained sourly, "which of course I have no intention of doing. Much more sporting to let the state kill me, wouldn't you say? And someone else can account for the sin."

"Indeed," Gabriel said. "Look here, I know you have no desire to talk to me, and I quite understand, so I'll get to the point. There is something I need to know and something you need to know."

Dr Paige stepped back warily and sat down, looking intently at Gabriel as he did so. "Not sure this is the time for riddles, Father. What the devil do you mean?"

"I mean that there is a piece of information I need from you, Dr Paige, before I leave you in peace to prepare for your trial. I am simply tying up a few threads here and there. But there is also something I need to tell you which may have some influence on your line of defence when it comes to it. Perhaps we could reach an agreement?"

Dr Paige looked away in what might have been disgust if he had retained the energy for such feelings. "I'll set my own terms if it's all the same to you, Father. You have my permission to ask me whatever you like, on condition that you swear never to approach me again. Is that agreeable to you?"

"Perfectly," said Gabriel, relaxing a little. He knew now that he would receive an answer, even if the man shouted it in his face with all the rage of hell. "Gordon Merriott . . . humour me, Doctor, I know your feelings about him. Gordon Merriott claims that some time before the murder, he was walking past your house and heard noises coming from your open window suggesting that you were hurting your wife."

"Father . . ."

"He said there was shouting and the signs of a struggle; your wife was pleading with you to leave her alone."

"Father, I have already explained this to Inspector Applegate," said Dr Paige, with a tone of complete resignation. "He wanted to know where Marie's bruises had come from. Marie was terrified of needles. Not in the way most people are frightened of them, I mean that the sight of a needle sent her into a state of utter panic. They were all like that, it made it very difficult to treat any of the camp survivors."

"I see." Gabriel noticed that Dr Paige always became more confident when he was talking about his own field. At the very mention of the word "treat" he had sat up straighter and stopped scrutinising Gabriel with his usual suspicion. "Perhaps you could explain?"

"The SS had many ways to commit murder, one of them was by injection," said Dr Paige. "It made it very difficult for doctors to treat the survivors afterwards. When a person is so badly undernourished, the first thing I would normally suggest would be to put them on a drip but the camp survivors used to become so hysterical it was impossible. Marie was just like that. We had to resort to Bengal Famine Mixture or milk just to get some nourishment into them, and it did not always work." Dr Paige looked at Gabriel and clearly did not like what he saw. "You don't understand, Father, no one does. When I say that Marie was frightened of needles, I mean the sight of them made her fear for her life. I didn't know what to do. She was too frightened to go to hospital—heaven knows how she will feel when she wakes up in one—she refused point blank to let any other doctor near her, so I treated her myself."

"Did you lose your temper that evening?"

"I raised my voice," he conceded, "and I regretted it almost immediately. I honestly *did* regret it."

"It's all right, I am sure you did."

Dr Paige began to fidget. "Look, this is hardly the time to feel sorry for one's self but it was awfully difficult. There are good reasons why doctors are told not to treat their own family. I had to look into my wife's eyes and see all that fear, knowing that I was the cause. It grated somehow, knowing that—even for a few short minutes—she could look at me and be reminded of one of her torturers."

"That must have been very hard."

Dr Paige sat up sharply, sensing a trap. "Distressing, certainly, but I would never have hurt her even in temper. On that occasion I restrained her but only because I was afraid she would injure herself. I did nothing to hurt her. When she had calmed down sufficiently I prepared her a sedative and —with her agreement—I waited until she was too groggy to mind before I gave her the injection."

"I see."

"Well?"

Gabriel shook his head. "I'm sorry, I forgot. I need to tell you something now, don't I?"

"You did say—"

"Yes, I did. Your friend Mr Brennan has spoken of confessing to the crime himself."

Dr Paige jumped as though Gabriel had struck him. "Are you mad? He had nothing to do with it!"

"How can you know that unless you know the real killer?"

Dr Paige threw himself at Gabriel, hurling him out of the way before hammering on the cell door. "I've had enough of this! I knew it was another trap!"

Gabriel backed away into the corner. "He has already tried to protect you once. He tried to hide the murder weapon when he realised it was yours."

"That gun was stolen from my house, it must have been!"

The door swung open and Gabriel scurried gratefully outside. "Thank you, Dr Paige, you appear to have an answer for everything."

"I will not deny it," said Gabriel, as he was escorted away from the cell by Inspector Applegate, "that was the first time in my life I have felt relieved to see your face."

"Delighted to hear it," answered Applegate, walking a step ahead of him along the corridor. "You may not feel so relieved when you see who's waiting for you in my office. I'd sooner be arraigned before the magistrate any day."

Gabriel had no need to enquire further; he knew precisely who would be waiting for him in Inspector Applegate's office and felt his entrails fragmenting into ice cubes as he stepped inside. There, larger than life and with a look fit to kill a man at ten paces, stood Abbot Ambrose. "No need to look quite so petrified, Gabriel, I am not here on your account," he began. "I came from the hospital a few minutes ago to tell Inspector Applegate that Mrs Paige has woken up."

Gabriel rushed forwards, momentarily forgetting his own position. "She's awake? Can she remember what happened?"

"Not a thing, according to the doctors, though that may change in time. At present, she is very tired and very confused. She cannot even recall how she came to be at the cottage." Abbot Ambrose turned to Applegate. "Perhaps you would be so kind as to inform Dr Paige of the good news."

"If it is good news for him," Applegate responded, "but I'll let him know anyhow."

"Thank you," said Abbot Ambrose. He gestured to Gabriel to follow him out of the room. "Good day to you, Inspector."

As soon as they were out of Applegate's hearing, Gabriel began making his apologies, but Ambrose silenced him with an impatient wave of the hand. "Not now, Gabriel, I will not listen."

"But Father Abb—"

"Do not imagine for a moment that I will forget your absurd behaviour in a hurry, but a few unfortunate people may require our assistance first. I'll deal with you later." Abbot Ambrose's manner was suddenly businesslike. "Now, perhaps you could tell me what you have discovered?"

Gabriel grasped the lifeline with both hands. "Well, Alastair Brennan is the man who wrecked the cottage. He discovered that Pederson was a camp guard. He found a painting of Marie."

"Ah yes, forgive me. My mistake. When you asked me whether Pederson and Mrs Paige might have met in the camps, I had forgotten that if one of them had been a guard, their paths might have crossed. Women usually guarded women, men guarded men but not always. As it happens, I have been busy conducting a little of my own research."

"About Pederson?"

"No, about Marie Paige." Ambrose returned Gabriel's perplexed look with a half smile. "I still have—friends—who know where to find answers, and I thought it best to check Mrs Paige's story. The fact is, now that Jerry is back in his box for the foreseeable future—please God—it has become fashionable for virtually everyone who lived under occupation to claim to have been in the resistance. In the end, very few ever were. If the numbers had been that great, there would have been no occupation in the first place."

"She was definitely sent to a concentration camp, she has the tattoo—"

"Indeed, but so many poor innocents were sent to perish in the camps that I thought it pertinent to find out why, especially as she was so young at the time."

Gabriel's heart had sunk so many times during his investigation that he barely noticed the response now. "And?"

"It turns out that her story is entirely correct. She was in the resistance, she acted as a courier. So she was not an actual fighter—though I don't think anyone ever claimed she was—but carrying messages about under the noses of the Germans was exceptionally dangerous."

"I suppose a young woman would have been quite useful for that," Gabriel observed before realising how it sounded. "I mean—well, you know what I mean."

"No cause for embarrassment. Attractive young women were quite good at distracting attention at checkpoints, I would imagine. Her codename was Firefly, apparently on account of her character."

Gabriel slowed down, ostensibly to catch his breath, but his mind was in a whirl again. "Why does none of this feel *right*?"

"Whatever do you mean? I've just told you her story is true. She *was* involved in active resistance, she *was* captured and tortured by the Gestapo, she *was* sent to the camps. What have your feelings to do with anything?"

Gabriel kicked the dusty road. "From the start, this has all felt so artificial and so real at the same time. Does that make any sense?"

"No."

"I can't explain it, it doesn't make any sense to me either. First of all we had Pederson, the Danish artist who was really a German artist named Weber. Everything about him was fraudulent except his being an artist, which was the detail that felt most artificial. Mrs Webb, the German refugee pretending to be Austrian, pretending her own son was a complete stranger—allegedly for a good reason."

"We do not of course know what she really knew about him."

"Of course. And then we have Paige, the kindly country doctor forever preoccupied with the care of his beloved wife. All his explanations are plausible—Marie's suspicious bruising *might* have been caused by iron injections, the screams and struggles Merriott heard *might* have been caused by hysteria—but it all feels so terribly convenient. Now it turns out that mousy little Marie really was a resistance fighter when I was beginning to suspect yet another cover story— how ever is that possible?"

Ambrose considered the matter. "I am not sure why she should not have been. What did you imagine a resistance fighter ought to look like?"

"I am still not making any sense, am I?"

"Not really, no. Perhaps if you were to slow down a little?"

"Forgive me, my thoughts are tumbling out all over the place." Gabriel decided to count to ten silently before continuing but could only bear to count to five. "I suppose what I mean is that, to have done all those things, she must have had an extraordinary nerve. I'm not sure I could have done it, constantly looking over my shoulder, knowing that if I made one mistake I'd be put against the nearest wall. Not to mention whatever happened to her after she was captured.

And if she was nicknamed Firefly, I don't suppose she was as mild as milk either. How did a character like that become the delicate, silent, bundle of nerves we know now? None of this feels *real*."

"That's a foolish observation," remarked Ambrose matter-of-factly, "the strongest will can be broken. If you had travelled to hell and back before you had reached your majority, you might also have suffered such a transformation."

"That's not exactly what I mean . . ." Gabriel petered out, hopelessly lost.

"I'm afraid you have exhausted yourself poring over the details of this nasty little puzzle," said Ambrose reasonably enough. "Your gut instincts do not match the facts, and your brain is going round and round in circles to compensate."

"Father Abbot, I know I have no right to ask anything further of you," began Gabriel after a judicious pause, "and I know I am in very serious trouble with you already, but might we go to the hospital before returning to the abbey?"

"They will not let you see her, Gabriel," warned Ambrose. "She is in a very weak state, in no position to have a conversation with anyone. Even if she could remember anything useful."

"I have only one question for her which will explain everything, and she may be able to answer it, even if she remembers nothing of the attack. It is the recent past that is hardest for a person like that to recall."

Abbot Ambrose came to a reluctant halt, which Gabriel prayed might mean he was prepared to make a detour. "There are still doubts in your mind about Dr Paige's guilt then?"

"Ten thousand difficulties do not make one doubt," answered Gabriel, "as Newman might have said. I have had just two difficulties to resolve before Dr Paige has his day in court. He has answered one of them, but I'm afraid only his wife can answer the other."

Ambrose looked ponderously into the distance. "I have no idea why, but I am inclined to listen to you on this occasion. However, I think we should go together."

Gabriel's relief was tempered somewhat by the thought of company. "Oh, there is really no need. I shall not be—"

"There is every need, if the past few days are anything to go by. We will go together."

Gabriel suspected, as they made an about-face for the hospital, that Abbot Ambrose would not trust him as far as he could throw a grand piano. All the same, Gabriel felt as though he were being sent on an errand under armed guard with Abbot Ambrose marching beside him with heavy, resolute steps, watching his every move. It was a good ten minutes before Gabriel had gathered up his nerves enough to speak again. "Father Abbot, when this is over—"

"When you have finished the journey you should never have embarked upon in the first place, we will talk further. I'm sure you understand. For the present, let us see about this last difficulty of yours."

The front of the hospital was quiet at that hour of the day. A young nurse was busily assisting an elderly gentleman down some steps, the man in question apologising profusely for causing her so much bother; on a narrow wooden bench to one side of the entrance, two patients sat taking the air. As the two men entered the hospital, Gabriel's attention was drawn to the sound of a car coming to a halt in the street behind them and he glanced back. He recognised the motor a moment before Inspector Applegate and a younger policeman got out. There was a short pause before they hauled out the unmistakeable figure of Dr Paige from the back of the car, his hands shackled in front of him.

Gabriel turned and bolted down the corridor as fast as his legs would carry him, leaving Abbot Ambrose and various assorted hospital staff to bellow at his retreating back to stop at once. He knew he could not stop. Even if it were the only way to prevent himself being thrown bodily out of the hospital and perhaps his own community, he could not stop now. He rushed up a flight of stairs, taking the steps three at a time and burst into Marie Paige's room without having the presence of mind to slow down.

Marie lay in exactly the same place Gabriel remembered from his previous visit, but this time very much awake and a great deal more alert than he had expected. At the sight of a vast figure in black hurtling into the room, she opened her mouth to scream, but to Gabriel's relief, he had succeeded in startling her so severely that she was too shocked to utter more than a strangled whimper. "Don't be afraid, it's me. It's Father Gabriel from the abbey." Marie stared at him, her face frozen with fear, but at least she did not attempt to cry out again. "I am terribly sorry to burst in on you like this, Mrs Paige, but there is something I must ask you before your husband arrives."

She continued to look blankly at him. "My husband is here?" she managed to say. "My husband? I . . . I called for him and the nurse said he was not there. She wouldn't tell me why."

Gabriel knew he was taking a gamble. Even wide awake,

144

Marie looked to be at death's door and her speech was hushed and laboured, but she appeared entirely *compos mentis*. "Mrs Paige, I have to ask you this. Why were you arrested? How did you come to fall into the hands of the Gestapo?"

Marie recoiled as though he had hurled a grenade in her direction. "What?"

"You were known as Firefly, you were betrayed by your best friend . . ."

"What do you think you are doing?" came a shrill, angry voice from the corridor. The matron Gabriel remembered from his last visit came striding in like an avenging angel, planting her stout figure firmly between patient and inquisitor. "How dare you come in here unannounced? The patient is very weak, she is not permitted any visitors. You had no right—"

"She is a good deal stronger than any of us have given her credit for being," Gabriel began, but entering into an argument with a hospital matron was tantamount to suicide. "If I could only—"

"Leave immediately or I will summon help." *Wonderful,* thought Gabriel, *that really will make the Abbot's day.* He had a brief vision of himself being bundled into the back of Applegate's car and the accompanying headline on the local rag: "Mad Monk Arrested at Hospital".

"Get out!"

"No," said a quiet, clear voice from the bed, causing the matron to turn sharply in Marie's direction. "I have to speak to him."

"Nonsense," retorted Matron, "I will not allow it."

"I will speak to him."

Gabriel watched the two women sizing one another up;

145

one a flushed, portly woman at the peak of her professional power, the other a shadow of a woman, still bearing the signs of an assault that had nearly killed her. It occurred to him, looking at Marie's impassively defiant face that she was not without fear; she had simply become so accustomed to being afraid that it had no hold over her any longer. "I will not allow you to speak to this man," repeated Matron in a tone that ought to have ended any argument.

"What are you going to do about it?" asked Marie. Her question would have been impertinent had it not been asked in such a calm manner. "What are you going to do to me if I speak to him? I know you can't hurt me, my husband has told me that hundreds of times: 'This is England, darling, no one's going to hurt you.'" She closed her eyes, apparently exhausted by the effort of a few minutes' tense conversation.

"Firefly," said Gabriel, "there is very little time. Please tell me how you came to be arrested."

"Why is it important?" asked Marie, without opening her eyes. "It was years ago."

"All will become clear, but I do need to know."

Matron was standing at the bedside again. "She is too weak for this," she protested a little more gently than before. "She must not become distressed."

Gabriel knelt down by Marie's head so that he could be as close as possible to her uninjured ear to avoid the need to raise his voice. "Marie, I'm not here to stand in judgement of you. You have nothing to be ashamed of."

"But I do," she whispered, "you know I do. That's why you have come." She did not open her eyes, but he saw tears sliding down the sides of her face before disappearing quickly into the folds of her bandages. "I was arrested because I did a bad thing. I was . . ." She opened her eyes as though to remind herself that there was somebody listening, but Gabriel felt as though she were looking directly through him. "I was only a messenger. They taught me how to use a gun because they said I might have to one day, but I . . . well I never wanted to hurt anyone. I felt such a frightful hypocrite because I knew the Nazis could only be stopped by force and I was aiding and abetting others to fight, but I never got my hands dirty. I never laid explosives or . . . well, you know what I mean."

"Not everyone has to shed blood, Marie, even in a just war."

"Easy enough for you to say," she persisted, taking hold of his hand, "the enemy was not living on your street. When the Gestapo came for me, I knew what I had to do. I shared a room with my mother, the pistol was always hidden in the same secret place. When I heard the door being kicked open, I picked it up and ran to the head of the stairs."

"It would not have been easy to shoot more than one of them without being killed yourself. They could've—"

"You don't understand at all. They were supposed to take me alive. If I had opened fire there would have been time for my mother to escape and I might have escaped myself, but I . . ." Her body began trembling so violently it looked as though she were convulsing.

"That's enough! Get out!" barked Matron, attempting to push Gabriel out of the way, but he was still kneeling and proved impossible to move. "She's had enough."

"I couldn't do it, Father, I couldn't pull the trigger!" Marie squeezed Gabriel's hand as tightly as she could, indicating to the Matron that she wanted him to stay. "I . . . I . . . knew what would happen if I didn't, but I couldn't fire and he knew I couldn't do it. He *mocked* me. 'Are you going to shoot me, little girl? Come on now, don't keep me waiting . . .'" She quoted her tormentor in the exaggerated German accent of a wartime propaganda film, mimicking the taunting voice of a man who knows he has absolutely nothing to fear. Gabriel imagined her, a terrified, shivering girl standing on the stairs in her nightclothes, making a last, doomed stand against a man who had the authority to liquidate her on a whim. "I just couldn't shoot him!"

Marie was sobbing almost inaudibly. Gabriel was aware of the presence of other people in the room behind him; he was not even sure how long the police officers, Dr Paige and Abbot Ambrose had been standing there. "You have nothing to be ashamed of, Marie," he repeated, pretending not to have noticed his audience. "There is nothing wrong with being unwilling to kill another human being, however wicked he might have been."

"An awful lot was lost because I lost my nerve," whispered Marie, "my mother had no time to escape. We were both taken, but they realised she was of no use to them and sent her away. She was killed at Ravensbrück."

Gabriel could think of nothing to say, but he did not need to. He felt a tap on his shoulder, commanding him to get up. "That's enough, Gabriel," said Abbot Ambrose. "You had better come with me."

Gabriel stood up as slowly as he could; he could feel his own pulse thundering in his neck and knew he had overstepped the mark so badly this time that even Abbot Ambrose would be unable to save him. He allowed himself to be escorted out into an adjacent room, where he immediately found himself facing a row of angry men standing in wait for him like a firing squad: Applegate, Dr Paige, the other police officer and, a moment later, Abbot Ambrose. He clasped his hands behind his back to steady himself. "I am sorry," he said slowly, glancing from one incandescent face to the next. "I am sorry for the distress I have caused, but I had to reach Marie before her husband could reach her. I have the answer I needed."

"Provoking that sort of response from a patient in such a fragile condition is extremely dangerous," said Dr Paige coldly, "you might quite easily have killed her."

"I wouldn't know how to do that," said Gabriel, looking Dr Paige directly in the eye, but the doctor did not flicker. "Perhaps you could educate me on the subject?"

"Be quiet, Gabriel!" ordered Ambrose, throwing him the most forbidding look he had ever received. "This has all been quite unnecessary. Dr Paige has seen fit to confess at long last."

14

"Do you understand?" asked Abbot Ambrose, when Gabriel failed to answer. "It's all over. It could have been over a long time ago, but at least now Dr Paige has chosen to do the decent thing."

"I knew you had," said Gabriel, turning to face Dr Paige. The doctor resolutely refused to look at him. "I knew you had," Gabriel repeated, "that was why I had to make a dash to your wife's bedside before you could reach her."

"I don't know what you're talking about," said Dr Paige, still looking away. "I was granted permission to see my wife because I confessed. I wrote my statement minutes ago, you cannot possibly have known anything about it."

"On the contrary, I knew as soon as you heard that your wife was awake that you would confess immediately."

"What if he did?" Applegate intervened. "He knew the chief witness was awake and might be able to give evidence against him if her memory returned."

"I couldn't bear my wife to be forced to do that after all she has been through," said Dr Paige. "If I came clean, I knew I could spare her the horror of standing against me in court."

"You sought to spare her a great deal more than that,"

answered Gabriel gently, "that is what this has been about all along, hasn't it?"

Dr Paige looked daggers at him. "I shot the man because he was attacking my wife. Any loving husband would have done the same—not that you would know anything about that."

Not for the first time, Gabriel felt a pang of grief he could only just brace himself to resist. "I do not doubt now that you are a loving husband," he answered, his voice trembling, "but perhaps it is about time you stopped coddling your wife as though she were a silly child." Gabriel stepped back in the direction of the door. "Inspector Applegate, Father Abbot, please allow me to explain."

"Don't let him anywhere near my wife!" protested Dr Paige. "The man's a dangerous lunatic!"

"That's not much of a diagnosis," answered Gabriel, turning to leave.

"I command you to leave her in peace!"

Gabriel stepped through the open door, glancing back to indicate to the others that they should follow. "Forgive me, Dr Paige, but you are not Marie's doctor, and she has not been your patient since you carried her to safety on that day in '45. You have no right to prevent your wife from speaking with me."

He had crossed the corridor and arrived back at Marie's bedside within seconds, but this time she saw him coming and regarded him quite calmly. "What's happening?" she asked. Marie's eyes were red and moist from her recent outburst, but she had gathered herself together with the swiftness of a woman who is used to sudden explosions of emotion. She looked over Gabriel's shoulder at the entrance to her room, and Gabriel knew the others were gathering there. "What's going on? Darling?"

Applegate and the other officer allowed Dr Paige to slip forwards and stand at Marie's bedside, hovering discreetly behind him as though they imagined he might make a break for it. "It's all right, my darling," said Dr Paige, leaning forwards to kiss Marie's face. "You're alive. That's all that matters."

Marie glanced nervously at the men who were so obviously standing guard over him. "What has happened?"

"Nothing for you to worry about," promised Dr Paige, "nothing at all. You just need to rest and get better. Don't —don't talk to these people."

"Marie does not have to speak to anyone," Gabriel assured him, standing opposite him across the bed, "but I suspect Marie can speak for herself."

Marie lay in stricken silence; Gabriel could sense the confusion churning round and round her head as she struggled to answer. He could understand why Dr Paige had always been so desperate to protect her. She looked like one of those ornaments made of finely spun glass that could shatter at the slightest pressure. With her hands clasped together over her chest, Gabriel could have counted every tiny bone in her hands and wrists. The stick-like arms disappeared into the generous folds of a hospital gown he suspected would have been too small for a healthy child. "Forgive me, Father," she said eventually, "but I am not sure what I am supposed to say to you. What on earth is going on?"

Gabriel pulled up a chair and sat beside her. "How much do you really remember of what happened?"

"Virtually nothing," she said. "I wasn't lying when I said

I had problems with my memory. My mind goes blank. It's
. . . it's like a curtain coming down. I know there's something I need to remember, I know something happened, but
I cannot see it."

"Make him leave her alone!" pleaded Dr Paige, looking
to Applegate for support. "I have already confessed to the
murder, what more can you need?"

"Father—" but Applegate stopped short at the sight of
Marie attempting to rise.

"But why?" exclaimed Marie, shocking the men into silence. She was hardly shouting at the top of her voice, it
was simply that no one had expected her to raise her voice
at all. "You didn't do it!"

"How can you know he didn't if you cannot remember
who did?" asked Gabriel. "And you do remember that there
was a murder?"

"Applegate, stop this!"

Marie struggled repeatedly to swallow. "I know there was
someone else," she managed to say. "It was not only me.
But my husband was nowhere near. I called for him. I called
—I called and called—he would have come if he had been
near enough to hear."

Dr Paige had apparently given up on receiving any assistance from Applegate, who stood in mute confusion watching the proceedings unfold. He appealed directly to Marie.
"Darling, you cannot possibly remember what happened.
You were beaten unconscious. The doctors say you may
never recover your memory. I killed Pederson because I believed he had killed you. Please don't think about it anymore, it will drive you mad."

Marie closed her eyes, clutching the sides of her bed as though she were clinging to a raft as it spiralled its way through a storm. "I know it didn't happen that way," she said, "but I do not know why."

"You know he did not do it," said Gabriel calmly, "because he could not possibly have done it." Dr Paige opened his mouth to protest, but Gabriel raised his hands in mock surrender, willing him to stop. "If you will allow me, Doctor?" Gabriel turned to Abbot Ambrose and Inspector Applegate. "Please, it might perhaps be easier if the truth comes from me."

"Inspector—" but Dr Paige lowered his head. "I really can't see the point in any of this."

"I realise this whole exercise may seem a little pointless," admitted Gabriel, "since it has appeared from the start as though Dr Paige here caught his wife in the act of adultery with Johannes Pederson. Gordon Merriott claimed to have heard a lovers' quarrel between Pederson and Mrs Paige; a note that looked to all intents and purposes like a love letter was found. Dr Paige's version of events, that he killed Pederson and that it was Pederson, in fact, who attacked Marie, makes a little more sense, but even then, there is a glaring problem."

"There is no—"

"Dr Paige, if a trained doctor really did shoot a man dead out of revenge for the murder of his wife, would he have left his living wife for dead and fled the scene? Wouldn't he at the very least have stopped to check for a pulse before running away? And if your motives were so honourable, why not confess immediately when the alternative was to be charged with the attempted murder of your wife as well as with Pederson's murder, not to mention being forced to bear the shame of your wife's affair?"

"Father, I did not know precisely what Pederson's dealings were with my wife—"

"Quite so. But your motive hardly matters since you were not armed to commit a crime and you were never at the cottage. I have a small confession of my own to make." Gabriel paused, hoping that Applegate and his Abbot would take it better than he expected them to. "I entered your house after your arrest, searching for clues."

"You broke into my house?"

"Not exactly. Gordon Merriott broke in. I found the door open and walked in. Anyway, I found there the chaos left behind by a man searching for something he suspects has already been taken. You owned a gun, you knew where it was stored. The only reason I could think of why you turned your house upside down looking for it is if you suspected it had already been stolen by somebody else. You were not searching for your gun that morning because you wished to use it, you wanted to convince yourself that no one else intended to do so."

Dr Paige was still reeling from the bombshell Gabriel had dropped on him. "I—well I don't think I could entirely forget where I had left it. I found it in the end."

"Dr Paige, you were nowhere near that cottage. The smallest, silliest little clue has been staring us in the face right from the moment little Jimmy burst into the abbey crying, 'Murder!' He said he heard a shot, but he did not see anyone leave the cottage. No one. It was assumed that he had had such a nasty shock that he was not thinking clearly, but I could not see how even a frightened child could fail to notice a person leaving a cottage that was so exposed. Like the abbey itself, it is not at all easy to enter and leave that cottage without being noticed—apart from some scanty undergrowth, there are no trees, no shelter at all in the immediate vicinity to hide behind. Jimmy said he saw no one leave because no one left."

Marie gave a low sigh. "Father, did everyone truly think I was having an affair with that thing? All the time I was in this hospital, is that what people have been saying about me?"

"You recognised that 'thing' at the garden party, didn't you?"

"Yes, that was why I fainted."

"And your husband did not want Mrs Webb to remove your jacket because he did not want her to reveal your tattoo. Did you recognise her as well?"

Marie faltered. "I know her from Mass if that is what you mean? Her accent always gave me the jitters, but she couldn't help that."

"You recognised Pederson then—Weber—as the camp guard who had singled you out long ago."

"Yes, I knew he had come for me." She opened her hand to reveal the jagged scar. "Perhaps he thought I was the only person left alive who could expose him."

Gabriel touched her palm lightly. "How did he do that?"

"He—" She closed her eyes. It was the moment when she might have been forgiven for breaking down, but no tears came. Instead, her pale face began to blotch red, as though her body was trying to blush but there was not enough blood in her veins for that. "He made me crush a glass bottle in my fist. It didn't produce enough blood so he had to pierce a vein."

"Alastair Brennan recognised your face in that picture. He realised what Pederson had done."

"Weber. His name was Weber." Marie looked wearily at him before shaking her head. "I'm sorry, but this is impossible."

"Let me tell the story," suggested Gabriel, softly, "then if you are able, perhaps you would be so kind as to fill in any details I omit?" Marie nodded. "Very well. When you received a note from Pederson—Weber—summoning you to his home, you knew he would never leave you in peace. So you went to the cottage armed with your husband's gun."

"If you knew the man he was, you would have armed yourself."

"This was not a mere act of self-defence. You went to that cottage with the intention of killing him. You only pretended to take your sedative on the previous evening so that you could be wide awake and slip out quietly before your husband was up. I doubt you slept much that night."

"I didn't."

"You could, of course, have gone to the police and had Mr Weber arrested as a war criminal."

"I hate the police." Marie opened her eyes suddenly and looked awkwardly at Inspector Applegate. "Sorry."

Applegate gave a rare smile. "It's all right. I'm not the Gestapo."

"I went to the cottage with the gun hidden in the inner pocket of my coat, but he—he was the one who pointed a gun at me. As soon as the door closed behind me."

"The presence of two guns was a little confusing," said Gabriel. "Of course, if the evidence had been properly in-spected, it would have been clear immediately that the gun picked up at the scene was not the murder weapon. Of course, it was not inconceivable that Weber might have kept a gun for the purposes of self-defence, even if he had never intended to fire it. The sight of a gun would be enough to deter most burglars."

"Not if one has seen rather a lot of guns over the years," said Marie, not noticing Applegate shuffling his feet at the unintentional put-down. "I suspected from the first moment I saw him at that party that he would try to hurt me. I went to sort him out rather than let him pursue me. I would have been driven mad otherwise, waiting for him to jump out at me, always looking over my shoulder, frightened to go out alone, frightened to answer the door in case it was him. It was easier this way."

"But things did not go according to plan. Something hap-pened you had not imagined could happen to you a second time."

Marie was weeping again, and no one tried to stop Dr Paige as he stepped forwards and held her hands. "You tell them everything," he whispered, "it can make no difference now."

Marie nodded in obvious relief. "Thank you. When I saw Weber pointing a gun at me, I was amazed at how calm I felt. I said to him, 'You're not going to shoot me. A bullet through the head would look too much like an execution. They'd realise who you are.' And he said, 'Of course not. In any case, someone might hear the shot.' The next thing I knew, I was on the floor, slightly stunned. I knew I had seconds to do it . . . my hand went to my pocket . . . but I couldn't."

"Like the previous time, you couldn't pull the trigger," said Gabriel. "You thought it would be different this time. After everything he had done, after everything you had witnessed. But your instinct was the same."

"It should not have been!" she wailed, "I owed it to the people he marched to the gas chambers—women, children. Mothers carrying their tiny babies. Father, they used to . . . the mothers would sing them *lullabies* . . ."

Marie sobbed against her husband's arm. Unable to embrace her because of the shackles Applegate had not seen fit to remove, Dr Paige pressed his face against hers so that their cheeks touched. "You know everything now," he said, without looking up. "I think that's enough."

"Wait a minute," Applegate interrupted. "If Mrs Paige didn't fire the fatal shot, then who did?"

"I didn't say she didn't," replied Gabriel.

"You just said—"

"But no one left the cottage." Applegate looked incredulously at him. "And it was all wrong anyway," continued Gabriel. "I kept thinking that, over and over again. Every detail of this sorry little mystery felt fake, it all felt *wrong*. Fr Dominic drew my attention to the nastiness of the murder. He said that whoever killed Pederson meant him to suffer. He was shot in the stomach and died a terrible, slow, painful death, possibly watching Marie being attacked as he died. Now that we know what we do about the victim, it is not unreasonable to suppose that the person who killed him hated him enough to make him suffer. But there were other, perfectly straightforward explanations—whoever fired the gun was an appalling shot or only pulled the trigger with the utmost reluctance." He glanced at Marie, who had lifted her head to face him. "In your case, Marie, perhaps both alternatives applied?"

Marie nodded. "It reached a point where I knew that I was going to die. One more blow might be enough. That was when I pulled out the gun and then I did fire."

"Flailing around on the floor, seriously injured, it must have been difficult to aim."

"I shut my eyes, Father."

The admission was so touchingly childish, Gabriel struggled not to smile. It was reminiscent of a little girl covering her eyes during a game of hide-and-seek, thinking it stopped anyone else from seeing her. "I see," he said. "Dr Paige, I think you had better retract your confession. Inspector?"

Applegate motioned for his officer to remove Dr Paige's handcuffs. "I could still find something to charge you with," he warned, "wasting police time for starters. I still don't see why you had to do that. Killing a man in self-defence is not a crime."

"But who was acting in self-defence, Inspector?" asked Gabriel. "That was surely your dilemma, wasn't it, Doctor?"

"Yes," Dr Paige agreed, rubbing his wrists absently. "I could not think of any other reason she could have gone to him armed unless she intended to kill him and premeditated murder *is* a hanging offence. It occurred to me that if Pederson had seen the gun as she stepped through the door, he might have attacked her to stop her shooting him. He might even have done it after she had fired the shot, given how long it would have taken him to die."

"He did continue to beat me after I had shot him," Marie

put in. "I don't think he saw the gun when I first arrived, but I will have to prove that at my trial."

"There won't be a trial, you're not fit to stand trial," Dr Paige insisted.

"But I want to be put on trial," insisted Marie. "Inspector, as soon as I am discharged from this hospital, I will come to the police station and you will place me under arrest."

Applegate clutched his head as though the room had started spinning out of control. "You know, never in my entire life have I heard a person demand to be arrested."

"Take no notice, Inspector," said Dr Paige, "she's not thinking rationally. She has only just woken from a coma."

"I know perfectly well what I am talking about," she said, pushing her husband gently away. It was a mild but unmistakeable gesture. "No one wants to talk about what happened. We've won the War, now we can forget all about it. I want people to know."

"There are other ways to tell that story," said Abbot Ambrose, who had been standing in silence all that time, observing the proceedings like a judge. "You need not put yourself through the misery of a murder trial for that reason."

Marie looked intently at him as though she had forgotten his presence in the room. "I know, but there is more to it than that. There is no point in fighting for justice only to run away from it. I have killed a man and I must account for that, even at the risk of being hanged."

The room descended into silence. Eventually, Applegate and the constable slipped quietly out and walked away down the corridor, followed shortly after by Gabriel and Abbot Ambrose. As Gabriel left, he glanced back at the bed where

Marie was drifting back to sleep, whilst Dr Paige sat at her side, tracing his fingers gently across the contours of her face. Gabriel knew he had no right to remain there any longer and that there was nothing further to be said. He turned and made his way noiselessly out of the room and out of the hospital.

15

Ambrose and Gabriel walked in silence through the village and along the familiar path to the abbey. Gabriel could smell rain in the air and wondered whether they would make it back to the shelter of home before the heavens opened. Not that he greatly cared; there was a gnawing anxiety in the pit of his stomach that was making him feel sickly and listless. "Penny for your thoughts, Dom Gabriel?" asked Abbot Ambrose, when they reached the abbey gate and Gabriel somehow found himself unable to reach up and open it.

"Will she hang?" he blurted out, pressing his head against the iron railings. "I can't bear the thought that that poor creature will hang because I found her out."

Ambrose nudged Gabriel gently away from the gate and opened it himself. "I think it singularly unlikely. I have a little more faith in English justice than you have, evidently."

"But even if she were to go to prison it would kill her."

"You may put your mind at rest on that score too. When Weber's history comes out in court, Mrs Paige will gain the sympathy of the jury fairly quickly, I suspect, and in the end, the prosecution would have to prove beyond any reasonable doubt that she committed murder when she pulled the trigger."

"But she meant to kill him! She went there with the intention of committing murder, it was premeditated."

They walked in silence past the cloister; Ambrose paused until they had begun to climb the stairs before responding. "The defence may argue that that decision was also self-defence. She believed he was going to kill her, she had experienced violence at his hands before and so took things into her own—a shaky defence, I might add, the law tends to take a rather dim view of rough justice."

"My thoughts exactly."

"But in the end, it is quite clear from her own account of things that she was only able to bring herself to pull the trigger when she knew with absolute certainty that she was about to be killed. She was right, one more blow delivered with the man's full strength, could easily have broken her neck or smashed her skull. The medical evidence will speak for her." Ambrose heaved open the door to his study. "But yes, she knows that, in theory at least, the outcome of the trial might be very grave indeed—but she is prepared to face that."

Gabriel followed Ambrose into the room, dragging his feet every step of the way. "She's a brave woman," he said to the world in general.

"The bravest of the brave. Or perhaps just honest." Ambrose settled himself at his desk. "As Mrs Paige told us, if one truly believes in justice, one must believe in it whether one is standing in the dock or the witness box. Or on the trapdoor with a noose around one's neck, I suppose." Gabriel's hand went reflexively to his throat. "Cheer up, Gabriel, I'd wager my own neck that Marie Paige will walk out of court a free woman. Eventually. Now, won't you sit down?"

Gabriel sat, watching as Ambrose opened a drawer in his desk and pulled out a cigarette case. The gesture could not have been more ominous if Ambrose had put on a black cap. "Not preparing me for my own execution, by any chance?" he asked, taking a cigarette out of the proffered box. Ambrose pushed a cigarette lighter across the desk towards him. "Why don't you just show me into a room with a revolver and a bottle of whisky?"

Ambrose exhaled slowly, watching the silvery wisps of smoke curling and dying in the air around him. "It's not quite that bad, old man, but I'm afraid there is something I must tell you and you will certainly not wish to hear it."

"I know."

Gabriel allowed himself to be distracted by the gentle patter of rain tapping against the windows. It seemed such a long time since the hot, sticky day of the garden party, when a lady's fainting spell could so easily be blamed on the weather. "I have been reflecting upon your future, Gabriel . . ."

~

Gabriel scooped up the four or five books standing neatly on his shelf and placed them carefully into the canvas bag lying forlornly open on his bed. It was the very same bag he had been issued when he had joined the army in the final months of the Great War. He had never intended to hang onto it, but when he had come to enter the monastery the battered, discoloured but serviceable relic of another life had served a useful purpose. Like a soldier, Gabriel had thought, a monk should carry around with him only what he truly needs.

Gabriel was just folding his pyjamas when there was a knock at the door. It was Dominic, wearing his customarily anxious face. He held out an apple like a votive offering. "You weren't at lunch," he said a little apologetically. "I thought you might like a bite to eat before you go. It's a long way . . ."

"Not such a long way really," said Gabriel, more to reassure himself than anyone else. "The parish is barely fifteen miles away as the crow flies."

"Still, an inch is as good as a mile, as they say."

"Are you trying to lift my spirits?" There were times when talking to Dominic really did cause Gabriel to lose the will to live. "Sorry, come in and sit down."

Dominic shuffled inside and closed the door. He paused whilst Gabriel removed his hat and coat from the chair before sitting down and watching absently as Gabriel laid out the offending items on the bed next to his bag. "You should have had some lunch, you know. You were missed."

"I don't have much appetite today. Not to worry, I shall feel better when I have arrived." Gabriel folded his tunic. A habit was not an easy garment to fold away but he made a sterling effort, taking an inordinate amount of time concentrating on aligning the seams correctly. He had changed into clericals earlier to put himself in the right frame of mind for travel, but all it did was to accelerate his yawning sense of apprehension.

"I'm sorry, Gabriel," said Dominic. "I'm sorry you are leaving us."

"Not forever, not for very long at all when it comes to it. Only as long as Fr Foley is convalescing." Gabriel's voice wavered. He could hear his mother many years ago, standing on the platform of the railway station, calling awkwardly to his seven-year-old self. "Don't cry, it's not for very long. Not long at all until the holidays . . ." If he thought about it, Gabriel had no idea how long he would be away from the abbey. He might well be asked to take over the running of the parish if Fr Foley was deemed unfit to continue following his recent heart attack. "I could be back by Christmas."

"Saint George's is a friendly parish, I've heard," volunteered Dominic, sounding like a spiv trying to sell his friend counterfeit petrol coupons. "You'll like it, you know."

"Father Abbot is quite right, I need some time away to reflect, I suppose. Though I dare say, I shall be kept busy." Gabriel opened the drawer of his bedside table and pulled out a large purple velvet pouch that might have looked on first inspection like a Bible concealed by a lovingly hand-crafted cover. The velvet was of fine quality, the seams embroidered with gold; Gabriel's thumb partially covered an initial embroidered in the same thread. "I suppose it is no bad thing that I should feel sad about going away. If the rule were so severe, I should not be able to leave fast enough."

"What's in there?" asked Dominic, pointing at the purple object Gabriel was tucking inside his bag with the tenderness of a mother settling a baby.

"A keepsake," said Gabriel absently, "well, a collection of keepsakes really. It wouldn't mean anything to you." He buckled the bag shut. "I'm not sure it should matter much to me either anymore."

"Gabriel . . ."

"You will make sure someone visits Mrs Paige, won't you? She may be in hospital for weeks yet."

"Of course."

169

"And someone should keep an eye on Mrs Webb. Her son may have turned into a monster, but he was still her son—she is grieving. And then there's Mr Brennan . . . oh dear."

"Gabriel!"

"So many casualties!"

"Naturally," remarked Dominic, standing up. "A man has been killed, a woman has been seriously injured. There were always going to be casualties, but that is not your fault."

"It still feels wrong to be walking away from them," Gabriel sighed, heaving his bag over his shoulder. "Well, not much I can do about that, I suppose." He had left his hat on the bed and reached down hopelessly to pick it up without having the presence of mind to put the bag down again for a moment. Dominic silently picked it up and handed it to him. "Thanks."

Gabriel was ready to leave but he hovered in the doorway all the same, searching for a reason to linger. "Do you happen to know if the car is ready?"

"Whenever you are," Dominic replied, stepping into the corridor in the knowledge that if he didn't move, Gabriel would never leave the room. "Gerard is to drive you over."

Gabriel smiled in spite of himself. "Marvellous! The way he drives, I may never need to settle into Saint George's." He turned at the sound of approaching footsteps and saw Abbot Ambrose moving hurriedly towards him. "I'm ready, Father Abbot," he said.

"Cheer up! You still look as though I'm sending you to your execution."

"The choice of driver would appear to indicate that,"

Dominic suggested, "The car has only just been repaired from the last prang."

Ambrose laughed. "Come now, that was hardly Gerard's fault." He nodded to Dominic, who stepped away discreetly. "It's all right, Gabriel, the choice of driver was quite deliberate. It is hard to be gloomy for very long in Brother Gerard's company. I thought it might make the journey a little easier for you."

"Much obliged." Gabriel felt the squirming urge to make a break for it that he would normally feel while seated in the dentist's waiting room or in the line for confession. It needed saying. "I'm sorry about the scrapes I got him into. I know I've said it before but when I'm gone . . ."

"No need to fret about that, Gabriel. Gerard's a grown man, he can answer for himself." He raised his hand in blessing. "Go safely now."

"Thank you."

Abbot Ambrose walked with Gabriel the short distance down the stairs and out into the tranquillity of a warm but sunless summer afternoon. They could see Gabriel's chauffeur some thirty yards away, sitting in the car clutching the steering wheel in uncontainable excitement. "Oh dear," said Gabriel, anticipating the screeching round corners and swerving to avoid pet cats. "You know, I could drive there and Gerard could drive the car back . . ."

At the sound of his name, Gerard looked up, grinned and turned the key in the ignition with an enthusiastic yank. The air was immediately polluted with the belching, roaring cacophony of a sad old car desperately battling for life. "She's more reliable than she sounds," said Ambrose. "Long may our transport last." He spun around to go indoors. With the Abbot's back turned and the noise of the engine invading his senses, Gabriel only just heard Ambrose's parting words: "I look forwards to welcoming you home again."

Gabriel slung his bag into the boot of the car and settled himself into the passenger seat. He closed his eyes and refused to open them until Gerard tapped him on the shoulder and informed him that they had left the village behind.